WHEN THE GHOST DOG HOWLS

GOOSEBUMPS HorrorLand™
ALL-NEW! ALL-TERRIFYING!
Also Available from Scholastic Audio Books

RIDE FOR YOUR LIFE!

THE VIDEO GAME
Available now from Scholastic Interactive

GET GOOSEBUMPS PHOTOSHOCK FOR YOUR iPhone™ OR iPod touch®

WHEN THE GHOST DOG HOWLS

R.L. STINE

SCHOLASTIC INC.
New York Toronto London Auckland
Sydney Mexico City New Delhi Hong Kong

ISBN: 978-0-545-16194-7

Goosebumps book series created by Parachute Press, Inc.

12 11 10 9 8 7 6 5 4 3 2   10 11 12 13 14 15/0

Printed in the U.S.A.   40
First printing, January 2010

PREVIOUSLY IN HORRORLAND . . .

Sixteen brave kids saved the park and managed to return home safely — but that doesn't mean the terror is over! The gates are open again — with all new stories, all new sights and frights. And while you're there, be sure to stop by Chiller House for a souvenir. A visit to Mr. Chiller's unusual shop will make sure you TAKE A LITTLE HORROR HOME WITH YOU!

PART ONE

"Andy, trade popcorn bags with me," Marnie said. She made a grab for my bag.

I swiped it away from her and spilled popcorn all over my lap. "Marnie — give me a break," I said with a groan. "Why do you want mine?"

"Yours looks like it tastes better," she said.

"Huh?" I squinted into my popcorn bag. "They're exactly the same."

"Then you don't mind trading — right?" She laughed.

My cousin, Marnie Myers, may be the grabbiest person in the world. And she always wants everything that's mine. But at least she has a sense of humor.

I like her laugh. She's twelve, the same age as me. But she laughs like a little kid.

She *looks* younger than me, too. In fact, even though we're cousins, we don't look anything alike.

She's short and thin. She has a narrow face with straight brown hair down to her shoulders and big green eyes.

Dad says I could be a middle linebacker. I guess that's his polite way of saying I'm big and maybe a little chubby. I have a round face with short black hair and brown eyes.

Dad says I always have a worried look. I don't think he's right. But yes, kids are always asking me, "Hey, Andy, are you okay?" when nothing is wrong.

Marnie and I get along really well — except when she's grabbing my popcorn or taking handfuls of French fries off my plate at lunch.

I handed her my popcorn. "Well? Aren't you going to give me yours?"

She shoved my hand away. "I have to taste them both first."

We were in HorrorLand Theme Park, sitting in the Haunted Theater, waiting for the show to start. The theater looked like a creepy, old haunted house in a horror movie.

The auditorium was dark, except for flickering candles on the walls. Thick cobwebs hung down from the balcony. Creepy organ music played. A skeleton usher stood in the aisle, holding a flashlight.

Suddenly, jagged lightning bolts flashed on the black curtain across the stage. And thunder boomed over the auditorium.

Behind us, a little kid started to cry. "This is *too scary!*" he wailed. "I don't *like* it!" His parents stood up, pulled him to the aisle, and led him out.

Marnie and I laughed. We'd been having good, scary fun all week in HorrorLand. Especially since our parents let us go off on our own most of the time.

Some of the rides were terrifying. And we both screamed our heads off in Werewolf Village. The half-human, half-wolf creatures were so *real!* Were they men wearing hairy costumes? The way they growled and snapped their pointed teeth, you'd *swear* you were staring at the real thing!

And another of our favorite places was The Game Preserve. Miles and miles of video games. Of course, Marnie had to play until she beat me at every game.

And now here we were, in the third row of the Haunted Theater, waiting for the show to start. In dripping green letters, a sign over the stage read: GHOST TOWN CLOWN SHOW.

Storm sounds poured out of the loudspeakers. Lightning flashed. Thunder boomed.

And I gasped as someone grabbed my shoulder and squeezed it hard.

"Hey!" I stared up into the face of a grinning clown standing in the aisle. He leaned over me and squeezed my shoulder again.

The clown's face was caked in white makeup.

His painted grin was crooked and smeared. He had a red bulb for a nose and a red-and-blue ruffled collar around his neck.

And as he leaned over me, I saw a hatchet buried deep in the top of his bald head. The blade was halfway in his skull. The handle poked up at an angle. Painted blood trickled down both sides of his face.

"Hiya, kid," he growled in a hoarse voice. "Let me introduce myself to ya. I'm Murder the Clown."

My mouth hung open. I wanted to say something, but I was too startled.

His breath smelled like onions. He brought his face down close to mine. And I could see that his eyes were totally bloodshot. And there were cracks all over his white makeup.

"Hey, kid — know why they call me Murder the Clown?" he growled.

"Because you have a hatchet in your head?" I answered.

His eyes bulged in shock. "I have a *what*?" he cried. "You're *joking*!"

Of course, he was being funny. So I laughed.

But he squeezed my arm and jerked me to my feet. "Come on, kid. Enough of this. You're outta here." He began to pull me to the stage.

I tried to pull back, but he was very strong. "Huh? What did *I* do?" I cried. "Hey — let go! Where are you *taking* me?"

2

Thunder crashed, shaking the auditorium. In the flicker of a lightning flash, I saw faces in the audience staring at the big clown and me. Behind me, Marnie jumped to her feet and made her way toward us.

"Come on, kiddo," Murder growled. "You've been volunteered." He raised both white-gloved hands to my shoulders and pushed me up the aisle.

I slid out from under his grasp. "I've been *what*?"

"You've been volunteered to be in the show," he said. "Fun time. You'll love it. Maybe you'll win a prize. What size clown costume do you wear? Are you a medium or a large? You're pretty big. I think I have an extra large back there."

"Wait a minute!" Marnie grabbed Murder by the collar. "Why does *Andy* get to be in it? I want to be in it, too."

Murder turned his watery, red eyes on my cousin. "I like you," he rasped. "I think I have a big nose that will fit you."

He gave us both a push. "Come on. We don't want to make the zombie clowns late for their meal. Know what they're having for lunch today?"

"No. What?" I asked.

"YOU!"

I didn't want to do this. No way. I'm kind of shy. Marnie was a *lot* more excited about going onstage than I was.

But a few minutes later, there we were in our red-and-white polka dot clown costumes. I had a big pillow tucked in my front to make me look fat and a stiff yellow wig that stood straight up in the air like a broom.

Marnie wore enormous platform boots that made her about eight feet tall. She had an ugly red smile smeared over her white face. Along with her polka-dot costume she wore a pointy red-striped hat tilted on her head like a dunce cap.

"Break a leg!" Murder whispered. He raised his big gloved hands and shoved us out onto the stage.

The show had already started. The lights were dim. Creepy music played. A ghostly fog billowed all over the stage.

8

Scary-looking clowns in drab black-and-gray costumes were doing handstands and somersaults in the fog. Marnie and I were the only ones wearing bright colors.

As I stumbled onstage, I saw a clown with a skull instead of a face. His ugly clown smile was painted in bright red lipstick on the skull. Beside him, I saw a sad-looking clown dressed in rags. He kept moaning and pulling out hunks of his curly hair.

The audience cheered as the clowns started to juggle. What were they throwing back and forth? It was hard to see in the fog. Were those shrunken heads they were tossing?

The clown with the skeleton face pulled Marnie and me into the circle of ghost clowns. Someone tossed me a shrunken head. "That's my Uncle Herman!" he shouted. "Toss him back!"

The head felt soft and warm. I tossed it back to the clown. Soon, Marnie and I were tossing the heads around with the other clowns. Faster and faster, till the audience cheered.

"You're doing great, kids," Murder the Clown called from the side of the stage.

But then I saw something that made me gasp. And that moment is where the fun ended — and the terror began.

In front of the stage, a fat clown was waving his hands at the audience. Suddenly, his hands vanished, and he waved with bony stubs. Then the hands returned. Then just fingers floated on the ends of his arms.

As I stared, the hands kept appearing and disappearing. Was the fog playing tricks on my eyes?

I turned to see what Marnie was doing — and saw a bald clown with sad black eyes lift his head off his neck. He tossed it across the stage to another clown.

"Hey!" I let out a cry. I gaped at the clown's stub of a neck poking up from his ruffled collar.

The second clown tossed the head in the air — and it floated above the stage. It bobbed high above us and didn't come down.

My heart started to pound.

Is this really happening?

Marnie put her hand on my shoulder. "Relax, Andy," she said. "It's all just part of the show."

"But — but —" I pointed to the headless clown.

The lights came on in the theater. I turned and squinted at the audience.

"Oh, wow," I murmured. "Marnie — look!" I grabbed my cousin by the shoulders and pointed.

When we were sitting out there, the theater had been filled with normal people. Kids and families.

But now, some of the people in the audience looked like creatures from a horror movie!

I saw rotting faces with missing eyeballs. . . . Heads with patches of hair torn away and bare skull poking out at the top . . . Missing arms . . . Open, toothless mouths with thick gobs of drool pouring over decayed chins . . . Shirts torn open and bloody guts dangling down.

"They look like GHOULS!" I cried. "Ghouls and zombies!"

And as I stared, the ugly creatures pulled themselves to their feet. And began to push their way into the aisles.

People screamed. Kids were crying. Some of the normal people grabbed their belongings and hurried to leave.

The auditorium filled with frightening moans and groans. The ugly creatures staggered toward the stage, eyes shut, arms stretched stiffly in front of them.

Marnie and I froze, watching in terror as the ghouls lumbered toward us.

I stared into the dark, empty eye sockets of a grinning skull — a ghoulish woman covered in crawling spiders. She tore out clumps of her hair as she staggered toward us.

"NOOOO!" I spun away. My eyes swept over the empty stage. "Marnie — the clowns! They all disappeared!"

Marnie and I were alone up there.

Bony green hands grabbed the edge of the stage. And then one of the creatures swung himself up. Groaning, moaning, they were all hoisting themselves onto the stage.

Holding on to my cousin, I took a trembling step back.

And heard the frightened voice of Murder the Clown from somewhere backstage.

"Malfunction! Malfunction!" he screamed. "Something is WRONG! Can't anyone SHUT THEM DOWN? The zombies are *out of control!*"

His terrified cry sent a chill down my body. I could tell it wasn't an act. The clown was really afraid!

More ghoulish creatures climbed onto the stage. Their heavy shoes scraped the floor. They moaned as if they were in pain.

As they staggered forward, their eyes were locked on Marnie and me. Their hands were outstretched, reaching for us.

We took another step back. I gazed around frantically. "Marnie — the stage door!"

We both took off toward the back wall. A narrow wooden door stood in the corner.

I grabbed the handle. Twisted it and pulled.

"It — it's LOCKED!" I cried.

I gripped the knob with both hands and shook the door with all my strength. It wouldn't budge.

The hideous, decaying creatures staggered closer. The air suddenly smelled like rotting meat. Glancing down, I saw a trail of yellowy slime on the floor.

Marnie pounded both fists on the stage door. "Open up!" she shrieked. "Open up! Can't anybody HELP us?"

A green-skinned ghoul, eyeballs rolling crazily in his head, stepped close. He rubbed his scrawny belly. *"Feed! Feed!"* he groaned.

He raised two fingers to his mouth and made loud slurping sounds, pretending to eat.

As they formed a ragged line in front of us, the others took up the terrifying cry. *"Feed! Feed! Feed!"*

Marnie and I had our backs pressed against the brick wall at the rear of the stage. As the disgusting creatures chanted and rubbed their bellies, we began to edge to one side.

"Feed . . . Feed!"

Slowly, we tried to slip away from them . . . sliding our feet silently over the floor, our backs pressed against the wall.

"HEY!" I uttered a cry as I tripped over something — and stumbled to my knees.

A big spotlight.

As I fell over it, the bright light flashed on. Right into the eyes of one of the ghouls.

He groaned and raised his bony arm to shield his eyes.

I grabbed the light by its sides. I raised it and aimed it at another green-faced ghoul.

He shrank away from the blinding brightness. I kept the light on him till he backed away.

My whole body trembling, I struggled to hold the big spotlight steady. I swept it over the line of moaning ghouls and zombies.

"Feed . . . Feed . . . Feed . . ."

They tried to shield their eyes. In the circle of bright light, they appeared to shrivel . . . shrivel and shrink. Moaning in pain, they staggered back.

"Keep it on them!" Marnie shouted. "It's working! Keep the bright light on them!"

I gripped the sides of the spotlight tightly. Could I keep the ugly creatures away till help arrived?

No.

I gasped as the light flickered . . . flickered and went out.

Darkness fell over the stage. The ghouls uncovered their eyes and pulled themselves up. They shook themselves. I saw an arm fall off and thud to the floor.

They began lurching toward Marnie and me again. They picked up their chant:

"Feed . . . Feed . . ."

Struggling to breathe, I shook the spotlight as hard as I could.

No. It was dead.

I let go of the spotlight — and felt a hand grip my shoulder.

Murder the Clown.

"This way," he growled. He pulled out a key and opened the stage door. Then he tugged Marnie and me through it. And slammed the door hard behind us.

I heard a squeal. A squeal of pain.

I glanced back — and saw two arms caught in the door. The fingers twitched. The hands didn't stop reaching for us.

"Feed . . . Feed . . . Feed . . ."

I could still hear the ugly chant on the other side of the door.

I swallowed. My throat was as dry as cotton. I glanced around. We were standing in a long, dimly lit hall.

"Quick thinking with that spotlight, kid," Murder rasped. "You held them back — at least for a while."

And then his watery eyes flashed, and he rubbed his gloved hands together. He leaned close and whispered in my ear: "You passed your first test. Now it gets REAL!"

5

"Huh?" I cried. "What do you mean? There's more?"

"Were those zombies real?" Marnie demanded. "Was it all a fake? Or were we really in danger?"

Murder the Clown tossed back his head and laughed. He winked at us. "Of *course* it was all a fake," he said. "*Everything* in HorrorLand is a fake — right?"

Then why was he sweating like that?

And why did he sound so frightened when we heard him pleading for someone to shut off the zombies?

He led the way down the long hall. "I was just kidding. You kids are finished," he said. "You did a great job. We gave everyone in the audience a thrill."

Was he *joking*? When the zombies and ghouls headed for the stage, most of the audience ran away!

Murder hummed to himself as he led us into a little dressing room. He helped us clean off the clown makeup. Then we climbed out of the clown costumes.

"This way, kids," Murder said. He led us to a shiny black doorway. "Glad you enjoyed yourselves," he rasped.

He started to open the door, then stopped. His ragged grin spread over his white-caked face. "Know why they call me Murder the Clown?"

He didn't give us time to answer. "Because I *murder* the audience!" he declared. "I really *murder* them!"

He chuckled to himself as he opened the door. "Don't let it hit you on the way out," he said. The door slammed shut behind us.

"N-now what?" I stammered. "Where *are* we?"

A bell jingled above our heads. I blinked in the bright light. It took a few seconds for my eyes to adjust.

The first thing I saw was a row of glass shelves against a blue wall. The shelves were filled with little dolls.

I took a step closer. The dolls had human bodies. Male and female. Dressed in dark striped business suits and frilly dresses in all colors.

Still blinking, I took another step closer. The dolls had human bodies, but their heads were strange. . . . They all had *wolf* heads!

Were they *werewolf* dolls?

"Check this out," Marnie said. She lifted a red-and-yellow package off a shelf. MAKE YOUR OWN QUICKSAND. The box showed a boy and girl up to their necks in yellow-brown sand.

Marnie laughed. "Look. It says you just add water and sand!"

"Kind of funny," I muttered. A slim green lizard with bright red eyes caught my attention. Was it made of rubber? Plastic? A sign read: GO AHEAD. PET THE LIZARD.

I reached out two fingers and gently rubbed the toy lizard's back.

"AAAAAAAIIIIIIIEEEEEEE!"

I jumped a mile as a deafening scream blared from the lizard's open mouth.

Marnie laughed. "That really gotcha, Andy! Ha-ha. I *want* one of those!"

"Is this some kind of joke store?" I asked.

We both turned and saw a blue-and-white sign above the cash register counter. In big drippy letters it read: CHILLER HOUSE. Under that it said: GIFTS & SOUVENIRS. ESTABLISHED 1496.

I rolled my eyes. "Yeah. For sure. 1496. Like I believe that."

"This store is awesome," Marnie said. She picked up a glass candy jar. The label read: SOUR GUMMI GERMS. "Check it out, Andy. I guess they're all shaped like germs!"

"Yum!" I said.

I glanced around. It was a small store. But it had shelves from floor to ceiling on every wall, and display counters and shelves stacked high in the middle of the room.

Things were piled everywhere. There was barely room to walk. All the shelves were jammed

21

with toys, and candy, and dolls, and scarves, and masks, and T-shirts, and all kinds of junk.

Marnie and I were the only customers. I didn't see anyone behind the cash register.

I picked up a box with a huge gorilla on the front. It said: INFLATABLE 800-POUND GORILLA. I set it down next to a giant shark jaw.

"Anyone home?" Marnie called.

Silence.

She cupped her hands around her mouth and tried again. "Anyone here? Is the store open?"

I heard a rustling sound from somewhere behind us. Then I heard footsteps. A man stepped out from behind a stack of boxes.

I blinked. He was big and balding, and he looked a lot like the drawing of Benjamin Franklin in our history textbook. Or maybe the old guy on the Quaker Oats oatmeal box.

I mean, he looked very old-fashioned.

He had little square eyeglasses perched low on his long pointed nose. He had pale blue eyes and thick white eyebrows. His thinning gray hair was swept back on his broad pink forehead and was scraggly in the back.

He wore a dark suit with a vest under the jacket. A ruffly white shirt and a black bow tie, big and loosely tied.

"Hello. Welcome," he said. He had a croaky old man's voice. When he smiled, a gold tooth gleamed in the side of his mouth.

22

He rubbed his hands together as if he were cold. He had long, slender fingers. I saw a sparkly blue-jeweled ring on one hand.

He stepped out from behind the boxes. He studied us over the rims of his square eyeglasses.

"Welcome to Chiller House," he said. "Allow me to introduce myself. I'm the owner of this shop, Jonathan Chiller." His gold tooth flashed again.

"Cool shop," I said. "Is that a real shark jaw?"

He kept rubbing his long hands together. "It's hard to say what is real and what isn't real," he replied.

He picked up a pink animal hoof and dangled it by the little chain attached to it. "Is this a *real* Lucky Pig's Foot? Or is it a fake?" He tossed it to Marnie. "I guess it comes down to what you believe."

Marnie examined it. "Well, it wasn't lucky for the pig!" she said.

Chiller's smile tightened across his face. He turned to me. "I see you're interested in the inflatable 800-pound gorilla. I have a good air pump to go with it. It only takes a few days to inflate it."

I shook my head. "I don't think my room is big enough," I said.

"This would make a nice gift for someone," Chiller said. He held up a wriggling brown thing.

23

"It's a two-headed worm. It's alive. I have plenty of worm food you can buy for it."

"Yuck," Marnie said, making a face.

Something caught my eye on a high shelf. I pulled it down. A large animal tooth on a leather cord.

"Is this from a jungle animal?" I asked.

Jonathan Chiller raised both hands, as if saying *stop*. "That's not really for kids," he said. "You might want to put that back on the shelf."

I stared at the tooth. "Why?"

"It has powers you may not want to unleash," Chiller whispered.

The tooth fell from my hand. I caught it by the cord.

Marnie laughed. "Chicken," she muttered.

"It isn't a joke," Chiller said. He took the tooth from me. He polished it with one finger.

The yellowish tooth had to come from a very big animal. It was nearly as big as my thumb! It was flat on the top except for a slender dent in the middle. It came down to two sharp points.

"Is it a tiger's tooth?" I asked.

Chiller shook his head. He pushed his tiny glasses up on his nose. "I'll tell you the history of this tooth," he said in his croaky voice. He began his story, rubbing the tooth as he talked.

"This tooth is more than three hundred years old. It comes from a tiny Highland village in Scotland. The people of the village were fishermen and sheep herders. Their village was a cold, bleak place. It was winter there six months of the year. They were cut off from the rest of the world — and very superstitious.

"One day, an unusual dog wandered into the village. The dog was a Blue Kerlew Hound. I know you've never heard of it. It was a rare breed of Scottish wolfhound. The hound's fur really was a dark shade of blue.

"The villagers didn't like a stranger in their village — especially a stranger with blue fur. And then bad things started to happen. The lake suddenly stopped giving up fish. And the sheep began dying from an unknown disease.

"They blamed it on the dog. They claimed the dog was enchanted and had brought the bad luck to their village. They tried to chase the dog away, but it wouldn't leave. They were afraid to kill it because of its evil powers.

"The desperate villagers sent for a sorcerer who lived nearby. They offered him the best house in the village if he could rid them of the dog.

"The sorcerer tried several spells to make the hound vanish. But the vanishing spells all failed.

"Finally, the sorcerer tried a different kind of spell. He cast a spell to make the hound lose all its teeth. He believed that would take the dog's power away.

"But the spell wasn't powerful enough. The dog lost only a single tooth.

"As the sorcerer watched, the dog uttered a howl of surprise. And then it turned and ran away. It wasn't seen again.

"People began catching fish once more. The sheep stopped dying. Good luck returned.

"The sorcerer was a hero in the village. He stayed in the best house, high on a green hill overlooking the lake.

"The sorcerer kept the tooth as a good-luck charm. To his surprise, he discovered that it could grant wishes. The tooth made him famous. Highlanders came from distant villages to have their wishes granted. Poems were written about the sorcerer and songs were sung.

"His story ended on a stormy, cold night.

"As the rain poured down, villagers heard horrible howls and cries from up on the hill. A flash of lightning lit up the sorcerer's cottage. Several villagers braved the rain to run up there.

"They found the tooth in a puddle of rain water. And they found the sorcerer dead. Torn to pieces. And then the villagers saw dog footprints in the mud surrounding the sorcerer's house.

"They knew that the Blue Kerlew Hound had returned for its revenge."

Chiller dangled the tooth in front of us. Marnie and I gazed at it silently. I guess we were both thinking about the incredible story.

I spoke up first. "How did *you* get the tooth?"

Chiller shrugged. His heavy suit made a scratchy sound. "I'm a collector," he said.

"The tooth really grants wishes?" I asked.

He nodded.

Marnie rolled her eyes. "Yeah. Sure. Like in all the old stories," she said. "It grants you three wishes — right? But the first two wishes don't turn out right. So you have to use the third wish to undo the first two wishes."

"No," Chiller said softly. "It's not like the old stories. The tooth grants ALL wishes. You just have to be careful of one thing."

He rubbed the tooth gently. Then he raised his pale eyes to us. "Don't let it get wet," he said. "The tooth was lying in a rain puddle. There's a lesson there. Keep it dry. Always keep it dry."

"What happens if it gets wet?" I asked.

"You'll get a shock," Chiller replied.

"A shock? What kind of shock?" I asked.

Chiller shrugged. He held the tooth up. It gleamed under the bright shop lights. "You still want to buy it?"

"I'll buy it!" Marnie said.

"Whoa. Wait," I said. "Give me a break, Marnie. I saw it first. I took it off the shelf. I want it."

Marnie stuck her tongue out at me. Then she turned to Chiller. "We'll *both* buy one!" she told him.

Jonathan Chiller swept a hand back over his thinning gray hair. "No," he said. "That's impossible. There's only one Blue Kerlew tooth in the world."

"I called it first. I said I'd buy it *first*," Marnie insisted.

"But I *saw* it first," I said. "Why are you such a copycat? Why do you always have to have what I have?"

That shut Marnie up. For a moment.

"Okay, okay. Fine," she snapped. "Take it. Go ahead, Andy. It's a total fake. You know it is. It probably isn't even a dog's tooth. I don't want it."

"Okay, great," I said. I turned to Chiller. "I'll take it."

He was already wrapping the tooth up in tissue paper. Then he placed it in a little box. He wrapped a blue ribbon around the box.

Then he took something from a drawer. A furry little figure. It was a tiny green-and-purple Horror, like the park workers in HorrorLand.

He attached the little Horror to the ribbon. Then he gazed hard at me and said, "Take a little Horror home with you."

I reached for my money. "How much does it cost?" I asked.

Chiller waved me away.

"No. No money," he said. *"You will pay me back next time you see me."*

I stared at him.

What did he mean by that?

29

PART TWO

8

Back home, I placed the little Horror on the top shelf of my bookcase. I didn't unwrap the tooth. I guess I kind of forgot about it. School break was over, and I had piles of homework to do.

The next Saturday, Marnie's parents dropped her off at my house for the day. She lives about twenty minutes away, so we're always visiting each other.

I don't mind. I told you — Marnie and I get along great. Except when she drives me crazy.

And today she was driving me crazy about the Blue Kerlew tooth. We were up in my room, and I wanted to finish my math assignment so maybe we could go to the mall or something.

But Marnie wouldn't let up about the tooth. "Where is it, Andy? Why haven't you tried it? Come on. Get it. Let's make a wish."

I pushed her out of my face. "It's just a joke," I told her. "You didn't really believe that crazy old guy's story — did you?"

"How do you know it's crazy unless you try it?" she asked. She pushed me back. "Come on. Just one wish. Where is it? Where?"

She reached for my shirt pocket. I tried to pull away. But she dug her fingers into my ribs and started tickling me like crazy. "Come on. Give it up, Andy. Where is it? Where?"

Marnie knows I'm totally ticklish. I struggled to squirm away from her, but I was laughing too hard to move. "Stop! Stop it!" I wailed.

She finally pulled her hands from my ribs. "Just one wish, Andy. Then I'll stop talking about it."

I squinted at her, gasping for breath. "Promise?"

She raised two fingers in the air. "I swear."

"Okay, okay." Grumbling to myself, I pulled the box from the desk drawer where I'd hidden it. I opened it and unwrapped the tissue paper.

Marnie made a grab for the tooth, but I swung it out of her reach. I slid the leather cord around my neck. Then I adjusted the big tooth on my chest.

Marnie shut her eyes. "Let's think. . . . What should we wish for?"

I squeezed the tooth in one hand. We stared at each other, thinking hard.

Downstairs, I heard my parents' voices. They were talking about dinner.

Without thinking, I said, "I wish we could go out for dinner. Mom's cooking is, like, disgusting."

Before Marnie had a chance to answer, Dad's deep voice rolled up the stairs: "Andy, are you ready? We're going out to the Burger Basket for dinner."

"Yessss!" I pumped my fist in the air.

Marnie's mouth dropped open. "Andy — you made a wish. And it came *true*!" she said breathlessly.

I blinked. "Huh?"

Marnie grabbed the tooth and squeezed it in her hand. "I wish I could go to the Burger Basket with you!" she cried.

And Dad called up the stairs: "Marnie — would you like to come with us?"

We were both so stunned, we burst out laughing.

"Is everything okay up there?" Dad called.

"No problem. We're coming," I shouted.

"The tooth — it works!" Marnie said, staring hard at it. "You squeeze it in your fingers and make a wish. And it works *instantly*!"

I shook my head. "It had to be a total coincidence. Don't make a big deal about it, Marnie."

I started for the door. But she grabbed me and spun me around.

"Let's make a big deal," she said. "Let's make a BIG wish. Something crazy."

"Not now," I said. "Mom and Dad are waiting for us."

She ignored me. "Let's see . . ." she murmured. "I wish . . . I wish . . ."

I clapped my hand over her mouth. I squeezed the tooth. "I wish Dad got a huge, brand-new red Escalade!" I exclaimed.

Marnie shoved my hand away. "Good one," she said. "Let's see if it came true."

We raced down the stairs. At the bottom, Marnie tripped me, and I nearly fell on my head.

"What's the rush? Are you two *starving*?" Mom called.

We ignored her and hurtled to the front door.

I held my breath. Was the tooth for real? Would there really be a new Escalade in the drive?

I pulled open the front door and leaped onto the stoop. My eyes swept up and down the driveway.

No.

No new car.

And then behind me, Marnie screamed: "I don't BELIEVE it!"

She grabbed my head with both hands and turned it to the street.

I uttered a cry when I saw a brand-new red Escalade parked at the curb.

"That's — that's *impossible*!" I stammered. "No WAY!"

Dad came up behind me. He had a big smile on his face. "Like it?"

"Well . . . YEAH!" I blurted out.

"The dealer is so desperate to sell it," Dad said, "he's letting me test drive it for a few days."

Marnie and I stared at each other. We were practically bursting. So far, the tooth had granted three wishes out of three!

I tucked the tooth down the front of my T-shirt. Marnie and I climbed into the back of the car. It was a real climb. The car was about a *mile* off the ground!

I took a long, deep breath. I love that new-car smell.

I rubbed my hands over the smooth leather seat. "Check it out, Marnie." I pointed to the DVD screen in front of us. "Is that totally awesome?"

"What movie should we wish for?" she whispered.

"Stop!" I said. I glanced to the front. Mom and Dad were fastening their seat belts. "Not another word about the tooth," I whispered.

Marnie stuck out her tongue. "Andy, don't you realize how incredible this is?" she whispered back. "We can have anything we want. *Anything!*"

"Why do you keep saying *we*?" I demanded. "Did you forget? It's MY tooth."

"I know it. So big deal."

"So stop saying *we*," I said. "I know you. You'll start making wish after wish, and I won't get a word in."

Mom twisted her head to the back. "What's that about wishes?" she asked. "What are you two arguing about?"

"Nothing," I said. "We *wish* we could decide whether to get fries or onion rings."

Mom laughed. "Why don't you get *both*?"

Marnie poked me in the ribs. "See?" she whispered. "Another wish came true!"

We sat in a big booth at the Burger Basket. Mom and Dad sat across from Marnie and me.

My dad is a clothing store manager, and he's a very calm, very serious person. But tonight he was totally psyched. All he wanted to talk about was the Escalade.

"I'm not sure we need such a huge thing," Mom said.

"Sure, we do," Dad insisted. "Look how easy it will be to drive the soccer team."

"But I'm not *on* the soccer team!" I chimed in.

"You might get on the soccer team *sometime*," Dad argued.

Good one, Dad.

Of course, Marnie and I were psyched, too. We were totally excited about the tooth. We were both *bursting* to tell my parents. But we both knew we had to keep it secret.

My parents don't have the greatest imaginations. If they thought I was getting crazy ideas about this big tooth I was wearing, they would definitely take it away from me.

The waitress took our order. Marnie and I both got fries and onion rings. Suddenly, my parents jumped up. They saw some friends across the restaurant. They slid out of the booth and hurried over to say hi.

As soon as they were gone, Marnie stuck out her hand. "Quick. Pull out the tooth."

"No way," I said. "They'll be back here in a second."

She wriggled her fingers toward me. "I'll tickle you. I really will."

I let out a long sigh. I pulled the tooth from under my shirt.

Marnie grabbed it. "I wish they bring me TWICE as many French fries as you!" she said.

"Nice," I muttered. I took the tooth back and tucked it away. "Do you really think you can use MY tooth whenever you want?"

"Yes," she said. "Don't be selfish."

We both sat there staring straight ahead.

Mom and Dad slid back into the booth. "You two are certainly quiet tonight," Mom said.

"We're . . . uh . . . thinking about homework," I replied.

The waitress brought the food. She set down the plates of French fries. Marnie got *twice* as many fries as me. She giggled.

"What's so funny?" Dad asked.

"So many fries!" Marnie said.

I rolled my eyes. Sometimes my cousin is totally annoying.

After dinner, we drove Marnie to her house. She opened the back door and jumped down from the Escalade. "Cool car!" she shouted to my dad.

Then she leaned back into the car and whispered to me, "Be sure to bring the tooth to school."

"Huh? I don't think so," I whispered back.

"Andy, just think," Marnie whispered. "We're never going to fail another test!"

She slammed the door and hurried up the walk to her house.

I sat back on the smooth leather seat and sighed. I suddenly felt very tense. My heart began beating fast.

I could feel the big tooth against my chest.

Was this thing too good to be true?

10

Later in bed, I couldn't stop thinking about the tooth.

Okay. I admit it. I don't just have a worried expression. I'm also a big worrier.

I gazed at it on the nightstand next to my bed.

Pale moonlight poured in from my open window. It made the tooth glow with an eerie green light.

I grabbed the leather cord and held the tooth in front of my face.

Do I really want to take it to school? I asked myself.

I pictured Marnie showing it off to all her friends. Strutting around. Acting like it was *her* tooth.

Then I pictured her friends grabbing for it, tugging it away, eager to make wishes of their own.

A riot with kids fighting over the tooth, battling in the halls, wrecking the whole school, making crazy wish after wish.

And who would get blamed?

Good old Andy.

A mistake, I thought, gazing at the glowing tooth next to me. *Bringing it to school could be a horrible mistake.*

I shut my eyes. And heard a howl.

"Huh?" My eyes shot open, and I jerked straight up in bed.

What WAS that?

I listened hard.

And through the open window, I heard a long, mournful howl. An animal howl.

Was it a dog? A neighborhood dog?

I've lived here all my life, I thought. *I've never heard a dog howling late at night before.*

The dog howled again, a long, warbling wail.

A shiver ran down my body.

Jonathan Chiller flashed into my mind. And once again, I heard his croaky voice telling the story of the Blue Kerlew Hound.

The mournful howls on the hill . . . The villagers running through the stormy night . . . finding the sorcerer torn to pieces. Torn to pieces!

Outside, I heard another sad animal howl.

I slid down under the covers. I shut my eyes.

43

And saw the big blue hound coming for me. It lumbered forward steadily with its tail raised straight behind it ... with its head high. Eyes glowing red as fire.

Howling ... howling as it came to tear me to pieces. As it came back for its missing tooth.

Another howl. Right outside.

So close ... so close. I pulled the covers over my head and pressed my hands over my ears.

But still I could hear it. Even under the covers, I could hear it howling ... howling into the night.

11

How much sleep did I get? Maybe an hour or two.

The next morning, I arrived at school with bloodshot eyes, yawning my head off. My head felt heavy, as if it were made of solid rock.

Sure enough, guess whose cousin was waiting for me at my locker.

"Did you bring it?" she asked. "Did you?"

"Good morning to you, too," I muttered. I turned the combination on my lock and pulled open the locker door.

"I'm not going to make a wish or anything," Marnie said. "I just want to show it to Judy."

I KNEW it!

"The bell is going to ring," I said. I squatted down to pick up books from the bottom of my locker.

"Did you bring it or not?" Marnie demanded.

I stood up and closed the locker. "Yes, I brought it," I said. "It's under my shirt, but —"

45

Some kids were watching us. I grabbed Marnie's arm and pulled her around the corner, out of sight.

"What's the big idea?" she said.

"*Sshhh.*" I raised a finger to my lips. "Listen, Marnie, this is serious. I mean, really. I heard a dog howling last night."

Her green eyes went wide. "So? You heard a dog. Big whoop."

"The dog howled all night," I said. "Right outside my window."

"Andy, why didn't you close the window?"

That's when I lost it. I grabbed Marnie by the shoulders. "Don't you *get* it?" I cried. "The Blue Kerlew Hound? Remember? They found the sorcerer torn to pieces? The dog came back?"

Marnie laughed. "You think the ghost dog came back to get you? That's nutty, Andy, and you know it. It was probably some dog down the street who didn't want to be left outdoors."

I let go of her shoulders. "Maybe," I said. "Maybe not. But listen, Marnie. Let's keep the tooth a secret, okay? I mean, for now. Making wishes is cool. But . . . I feel kind of creeped out about it."

She tugged the leather cord around my neck. "Well . . . if you don't want the tooth, you could give it to me. I mean, if you're totally stressed about it, I'd be happy to take it."

46

I slapped her hand away. "You never give up — do you!" I said. "Listen, I'm keeping the tooth. I just want to be careful, that's all."

"Okay, okay." Marnie rolled her eyes. "No problem. We'll be careful."

"Good," I said. I let out a long sigh and started to relax.

And that's when Marnie grabbed the cord. She pulled the tooth out from under my shirt and squeezed her hand around it.

Her green eyes flashed. A devilish grin spread over her face. And she called out, "I wish . . . I wish school will get out early because there's a *cow* loose in the building!"

"NO!" I cried. "Are you CRAZY?" I pried the tooth from her hand and started to jam it back into its hiding place under my shirt.

But sure enough, somewhere down the hall I heard some kids screaming. Then . . . running footsteps.

And then: *MOOOOOOOOOOOOO.*

12

Sunday afternoon, Mom dropped me off at the Cloverfield Mall. She said I could buy my own sneakers, as long as I didn't buy the ones with lights that flash when you walk.

I said no problem. Why would I buy baby sneakers, anyway?

But today was a big deal. She was actually trusting me to shop on my own.

As I started out of the car, she tucked a ten-dollar bill into my shirt pocket. "You didn't have much lunch, Andy. Buy yourself a snack."

Then she made a face. "Why do you insist on wearing that ugly tooth everywhere?"

I shrugged. "Dunno. It's like a good-luck thing." I slid out of the Escalade and waved good-bye.

I had no way of knowing that the tooth would *not* bring me good luck that day.

The mall was really crowded. A high school

band was playing in the rotunda. And across from it, a big mob gathered around a totally awesome sports car being auctioned off.

I tried to push my way to the front to get a better look. But I felt a hand on my shoulder. And a familiar voice said, "Why don't you trade the Escalade for the cool sports car?"

I let out a groan. "Marnie, how did you know I'd be here?" I asked.

Marnie wore a pale blue sweater and a short denim skirt over blue tights. She had a blue headband in her brown hair.

She grinned. "I'm psychic," she said. "Didn't you know I can read minds?"

"Really? What am I thinking right now?" I demanded.

She closed her eyes and concentrated. "You're thinking you want to use the tooth to get me all kinds of cool stuff at the mall today."

I burst out laughing.

"I'm serious," she said. She had her eyes on the tooth. "Let's see what we can wish for."

"Let's not," I said. I turned and started walking toward Shoe Universe.

She hurried after me. "Andy, you're no fun. We haven't had any fun at all with the tooth," she complained.

"Stop saying *we*," I said.

She made a pouty face. "Okay, okay."

"I don't think it should be used for fun," I told her. "The tooth is serious. It's kind of scary. It's like . . . having too much power."

"We could just get some little things," she said. She inhaled deeply. "*Mmmmm*. Those cinnamon buns smell so great!"

"My dad says it's a trick," I said. "He said they pipe that cinnamon smell out into the mall to get you to stop and buy one of their buns."

"I don't care," Marnie said. "How about wishing for cinnamon buns? One for each of us. That's not too scary — is it?"

"Here," I said. I pulled the ten-dollar bill from my pocket. "Mom gave me this for snacks. We can *buy* two cinnamon buns."

Marnie made her pouty face again. "That's a lot of fun. *Not*."

We walked past the Cineplex. Three teenage dudes were arguing with the girl in the glass ticket booth that they were old enough to go into some movie. It must have been R-rated. The girl kept shouting, "Just show me your ID!" over and over.

"How about free movie tickets?" Marnie asked.

I shook my head. "No way. I'm here to buy sneakers."

"Why don't you just wish for the sneakers?"

"I want to pick them out."

"How about just one crazy wish, Andy? You know. Something insane. Like a cow loose in the mall."

I sighed. "Give me a break, Marnie. You already did that — remember?"

"And it was awesome!" she said, giggling.

"No more cows," I muttered.

Marnie took off toward her favorite store, Boutique Boutique. The sign in the window said: SO NICE WE NAMED IT TWICE. She nearly collided with two women pushing baby strollers.

"Andy, check it out."

I made my way slowly up to the shop window. Marnie had her face to the glass, staring at a pile of sweaters. A little sign read: PURE CASHMERE.

"Don't drool," I said. "It's very immature."

She shoved me hard in the ribs. "I just want the blue one and the pale green one," she said. "Or maybe the creamy white one."

She turned to me. "I'm really not into sweaters, but those are amazing. Please, Andy? It's so simple. Just make a wish for me to have two of them in my size? What can it hurt?"

I'd been pretty calm and patient. But she grabbed my shoulders and started shaking me and begging, "Please? Pretty please . . . ?"

And that's when I lost it. And I screamed, "You're driving me CRAZY! I wish you'd STOP TALKING about the tooth!"

51

Marnie made a hard swallowing sound. Like she was choking.

Then she moved her lips — and no sound came out.

"What's wrong?" I asked. "I can't hear you."

Her face turned red. I could read her lips: "I ... can't ... talk. I ... can't ... talk!"

She couldn't make a sound — not even a whisper.

I stared hard at her. "You're joking — right?"

She shook her head. Her eyes bulged. I could see she was trying to shout.

But no sound came out.

She really couldn't speak.

A chill ran down my back. My mouth dropped open in fright.

What have I DONE?

13

Marnie waved her hands frantically. She struggled to speak, to make a sound. A hoarse bleat escaped her throat, and she started to cough.

My mind whirred from thought to thought:

Serves her right. She was making me NUTS wishing for everything she saw.

But then I thought:

This is terrible! What if she can never speak again? What if I've ruined her life?

She tugged my sleeve with one hand and pointed wildly to her throat with the other. I couldn't read her lips. But I knew what she wanted. She wanted me to wish her voice back.

"Okay," I said.

But she grabbed the tooth before I had a chance. She tugged it really hard.

"OUCH!" I let out a scream as the leather cord dug into my neck. "Hey — you CUT me!" I rubbed the side of my neck where it throbbed. "Is it bleeding?"

Marnie scowled at me. With a deep sigh I grabbed the tooth and made the wish for her.

"Yes!" she cried. "It's back. My voice — I can talk again!" She gave me a hard punch on the shoulder. "How could you DO that to me?"

"I . . . I didn't mean to," I stammered. "It was a total accident. But you asked for it, didn't you?"

She started to sing at the top of her lungs. "I love my voice!" she said when she finally finished. "It's beautiful!"

I pressed one hand against my neck. "Look what you did to me. Is there a bruise? Is it bleeding?"

She tilted my head to one side. "It's a little cut," she said. "Just a tiny drip of blood." She wiped it with her fingers. "Sorry. I didn't mean to cut you. It was an emergency."

"Emergency?" I cried. "It wouldn't be an emergency if you didn't drive me crazy with all your wishes. If — if —"

I stopped. People were staring at us. I recognized two kids from school. They were pointing at us and laughing.

I spun away and started to walk. "Let's go," I said. "Shoe Universe is around the corner. Are you coming with me?"

She trotted after me. "Tell you what," she said. "I'll make you a deal."

54

I shook my head. "No deal."

"Andy, you're being a total jerk," she said.

"Stop trying to get on my good side," I said.

"One wish," Marnie said. "That's all. Come on. One wish — and I'll shut up. I won't even mention the tooth for the rest of the day."

I turned to face her. "How about for the rest of the week?"

"Promise," she said.

"If we do one wish, you promise you won't say the word *tooth* for a week? Raise your hand and swear."

"I swear," Marnie said. "But it has to be a good wish."

"Okay. Deal," I said. We were standing outside Shoe Universe. I pulled the leather cord over my head. I held the big tooth in front of me.

"Let *me* make the wish," Marnie said. She grabbed for the tooth — and it fell out of my hand.

"Get back," I said. I leaned down. The tooth had landed in some kind of sticky puddle. It looked like orange soda.

I picked it up and wiped it with my hand. "Here goes," I said.

Marnie's eyes flashed eagerly. She had an excited grin frozen on her face.

I took a deep breath. "I wish for Shoe Universe to give you and me *free pairs* of their absolutely most awesome sneakers!"

I waited. I realized I was still holding my breath.

I heard a buzzing sound. It sounded like a hive of bees all buzzing at once.

It took me a few seconds to realize the tooth was buzzing. And then it started to vibrate in my hand. Harder . . . harder . . . until it made my hand ache.

"Huh?" I uttered a confused gasp.

A blinding light made me shut my eyes.

Marnie screamed.

A white bolt of electricity roared over me.

I didn't even realize I was dancing. Caught in the jolting electricity, my body twisted and jerked.

My arms flew over my head. My legs did a wild jig.

The loud buzzing no longer surrounded me. It was in my head now. Like a thousand bees, buzzing . . . bumping against my brain . . . bumping me as I danced in the painful current.

And then, nothing. Just silent darkness.

14

My eyes slowly filled with light. As if someone were lifting a window shade in front of my face.

I heard myself groan. My head throbbed. I could feel the blood pulsing at my temples.

I shut my eyes and saw flashing red lights.

"Andy?" A voice called my name from somewhere far in the distance. The red lights faded to gray.

"Andy? Are you waking up?"

I blinked, letting in the bright light again. Why did my head hurt so much? Why did my whole body ache?

I felt as if I could feel every one of my bones.

"He's opening his eyes," a girl said. Was it Marnie?

"He's coming around." Another voice, still far away. Mom?

My body twitched. My mouth opened with a gurgling sound.

I tried to sit up. But a shock of pain to my head made me drop back down.

"Where am I?"

Was that *my* voice? So hoarse and husky.

I blinked a few more times. I saw a red ceiling light. And then green curtains blowing at an open window.

My room?

No. The colors were all wrong. I didn't have a red ceiling light and green curtains.

Brown eyes floated over me behind black eyeglasses. Thinning brown hair. A bushy brown mustache.

"Hello?" I uttered. "Where am I?"

"Don't you recognize me?" the man said, his face hovering over mine. "I'm your dad."

I made a choking sound. "My dad? No you're not."

"Give him some air," a woman said. She pulled the man back from my bed.

I groaned again. Marnie sat by the bed, looking very tense and pale.

"Marnie — where am I? Who are these people?" I asked.

"They're your parents," she whispered.

"But I've never seen them before!" I cried.

"Just be calm. You're safe and sound," the woman said. She smoothed her warm hand over my forehead, brushing my hair up.

"You had a bad shock," Marnie said. "At the mall."

The man turned to the woman. "Did he fry his brain?" he asked her in a loud whisper. "Did he fry it?"

"They think you fried your brain," Marnie said.

"No!" I cried. A stab of pain made me cringe. "My brain is okay. But I don't know these people!"

A blond-haired little girl poked her face over mine. "Andy, are you faking?" she demanded.

"Huh? Faking? Who are you?" I cried.

She rolled her eyes. "Your sister, of course. Don't you remember me? Margaret? But you call me Muggy?"

"Muggy?"

My mouth was suddenly too dry to talk. My heart pounded.

I didn't remember her. I didn't remember any of them, except for Marnie.

Did I fry my brain? Was my memory wrecked?

The red ceiling light started to spin. The bed tilted. I grabbed the sheets to keep from falling out.

"Marnie — help me!" I cried. "Help me remember. I don't know these people."

"Is his brain fried?" the man repeated. "Is it fried?"

The little girl pushed her face up to mine and started to sing: *"Muggy Muggy Muggy, you're so Uggy Uggy Uggy!"*

She poked me in the ribs. "Don't you remember that song? You made it up? You always sing it to make me mad?"

"I — I don't remember," I choked out. "I — I'm so sorry, everyone. I don't remember you. I really don't."

"The tooth was wet," Marnie said. "Jonathan Chiller said you'd get a shock. You didn't dry off the tooth, Andy. And you fried your brain."

"NO — PLEASE!" I cried. "DON'T SAY THAT!"

"He fried it," the man said to the woman. They both shook their heads. "He fried it."

The little girl pinched my shoulder really hard. *"Muggy Muggy Muggy, you're so Uggy Uggy Uggy!"*

"Stop — please!" I moaned. "Stop singing that."

"I'm going to sing it till you remember me!" she said. She pinched me again. Pain shot down my body.

"Muggy Muggy Muggy, you're so Uggy Uggy Uggy!"

"Don't you see?" Marnie said. "The tooth was wet. You made a wish when the tooth was wet."

"And you fried your brain," the man said. "I'm your dad. And I'm telling you the truth. You fried it."

"NOOOO!" I let out a howl. "You're not my dad! And you're not my mom! And I don't have a sister! This is *crazy*!"

I grabbed my head with both hands and screamed: "I — I wish I was ten thousand miles away from all of you!"

And: *RRRRRRRRRRRIPPPPPPP!*

I heard a loud *ripping* sound, like someone tugging open a Velcro shoe.

And then I felt myself being ripped away — torn from the bed . . . from the strange room. Ripped away as if pulled by a powerful vacuum cleaner.

I shut my eyes.

Was that ME screaming?

RRRRRRRRRRRIPPPPPPP. The sound followed me.

I landed with a jolt on something hard. My eyes shot open.

I blinked, struggling to focus. Where was I?

I was buckled into a hard metal seat. Staring out a wide window. Staring out into darkness.

No. As my eyes adjusted, I saw twinkling stars. Millions of twinkling stars.

And then a planet floated into view far above me. A green-and-blue planet. It took me a while to recognize the shape — and then I gasped.

I swallowed hard. My breath caught in my throat.

What was EARTH doing way out there?

15

My seat bounced. I glanced down and saw some kind of control panel spread out in front of me.

Lights blinked. Numbers flashed on LED screens. Computer monitors showed views of the stars outside.

I gazed from the controls to the floating ball that was Earth, high outside the window. It took me a long while to realize I was in some kind of space capsule.

My heart pounded. I gripped the sides of the chair so hard, my hands ached.

And I stared into the black depths of space all around me. The blinking stars were tiny bright dots, like pinpricks against the blackness.

Am I really ten thousand miles from Earth?

The question repeated in my mind.

Impossible. Impossible.

But here I was. I wished it — and here I was.

All alone, floating in outer space.

Chill after chill rolled down my back.

Was I afraid? Yes. Of course.

I grabbed for the tooth on the cord around my neck. I was ready to wish myself back home.

But I stopped myself. I was too dazzled by the awesome view.

I couldn't breathe. I couldn't move. I couldn't take my eyes off our blue-and-green planet.

How many people were lucky enough to see Earth this way?

"Wow," I said out loud, "I wish Marnie could see this."

I didn't think. I didn't mean to make a wish. The words just burst from my mouth as I gazed out the capsule's window. And . . .

RRRRRRRRRRRIPPPPPP.

That sound again. Like someone tearing fabric.

The capsule rocked. I was tossed forward, then back.

Marnie popped into the seat beside me. She bounced once, then settled on the metal chair.

"NOOOO!" She uttered a frightened cry. Her eyes bulged at the view out the window.

And then she saw me beside her. "Andy? Where ARE we?" she asked in a tiny voice.

"Outer space," I said. I pointed toward Earth floating above us.

"NO!" Marnie cried again. "You wished . . . ?"

I nodded. "I wished for you to see this, too," I said. "Isn't it amazing?"

"No! It's *not*!" she cried. "I don't like it, Andy.

I don't want to be in outer space! Why did you do this to me? Why?"

"I told you —"

"Get us back!" Marnie screamed. "I don't want to be here. You KNOW I'm afraid of flying!"

"Huh? Flying?"

"I am *terrified*. Do you understand?" Her whole body trembled. Her eyes rolled crazily in her head.

"Marnie, don't freak," I said. "Take a deep breath. Look how awesome it is!"

"I don't want to look!" she wailed, covering her eyes. "Get us home, Andy! Get us home! Get us home!"

She started pounding the control panel with both fists. "Get us home! Get us home!" She was going totally berserk.

"Okay!" I cried.

But before I could make a wish, she turned and grabbed the cord around my neck. She swung her hand up and pulled the tooth over my head.

"Give it back!" I cried. I made a grab for it — and *it floated out of Marnie's grasp.*

"It — it's weightless!" I stammered.

I made another grab. Missed.

The tooth floated higher, toward the ceiling of the capsule.

Marnie unbuckled her seat belt. She floated out of her chair. She reached out both hands and swiped at the tooth.

Missed.

The tooth floated higher. Toward some kind of air vent.

I unbuckled myself, kicked off — and went sailing up out of my chair. I floated toward the top of the capsule — and dove for the tooth.

My fingers wrapped around it. But the tooth slid right through them and sailed higher.

Marnie and I bumped heads.

"OW!" I cried. "Look out!"

"How can I look out?" Marnie cried. "I've never flown before."

"It's going into that vent!" I cried. We both stretched our arms out, trying to fly higher.

"Yes!" I shouted as I grabbed the tooth and pulled it down to me.

But Marnie and I flew into each other again. My arms got tangled in hers. We struggled to pull apart.

I gasped. "We're upside down!"

Marnie tried to swing herself around — and kicked me in the chest.

Now we were both sailing down headfirst.

"Can't . . . turn . . . around . . ." I said. And then my head bumped the control panel. *"Ouch!"*

I heard another *thud*. Marnie winced as she bumped the panel, too.

The whole capsule jerked and tilted from side to side.

And then I could feel it start to fall.

Floating in front of the window, I felt a strong pull against me. Like a magnet pulling me down.

"We're dropping!" I cried.

Out the window, I could see the blue-and-green ball of Earth appear to grow larger.

The capsule picked up speed as it fell. Faster . . . faster. I could feel the pressure. Feel the incredible pull.

It felt like someone was trying to pull my skin off! I couldn't move . . . couldn't breathe.

The Earth rose up in front of us, bigger . . . BIGGER.

"We're falling FAST!" Marnie shrieked. "We're going to crash!"

I gaped in horror as our planet filled the whole window.

The tooth. Andy, the tooth.

The words flew through my brain. In my total panic, I'd forgotten about it.

I had it gripped tightly in my fist.

I squeezed it hard. I struggled to breathe. I couldn't think straight.

We were hurtling toward Earth. About to smash into the planet.

I pictured us crushed, like an egg tossed against a brick wall.

What should I wish for?

"I — I wish I was back in my own bed!" I choked out.

Will it work?

16

RRRRRRRRRRRIPPPPP.

I heard the sound again. And felt myself being *snapped* away.

A bright whir of dancing colors flew past my eyes. They spun so fast, they made me dizzy.

I clamped my eyes shut.

And felt a hard *thud*. The landing knocked my breath out.

Choking, I opened my eyes. And stared up at solid blue.

It took me a long moment to realize I was lying in bed. My head rested on a pillow. The covers were pulled up to my chin.

A black-and-red bedspread. MY bedspread.

Yes! The tooth had come through again and granted my wish. I was definitely in my own bed.

But where was I?

I stared up at the solid blue. A pale, white cloud floated into view.

The sky. I was gazing up at sky.

How did my bed get *outdoors*?

I pushed down the bedspread, swung my feet to the ground, and sat up.

My eyes focused on a curtain of metal bars. A wall of thin bars, rising up high above my head.

Cage bars?

Yes. I twisted around and gazed behind me. Bars all around. A cage. I was in a large cage.

The ground was soft black dirt. I saw leafy trees inside the cage.

"Huh?" With a gasp, I jumped to my feet. My heart began to race in my chest.

The cage was huge. Bigger than my front yard. I saw a tire swing hanging from a limb of a tree. A row of tall bushes. A red-and-blue beach ball rested in a big sandbox, like you see in kiddie playgrounds.

"What's up with this?" I said out loud.

I took a few steps across the dirt — and realized I wasn't alone.

Eyes stared in at me from the other side of the cage bars.

I gasped when the faces came into focus. People were staring into the cage . . . staring at ME!

Was I in a zoo?

I saw about a dozen people. Some of them had goofy grins on their faces. They stared in at me, and poked each other, and giggled and pointed.

Were they *laughing* at me?

I struggled to get over my shock. "Hey!" I shouted. "Hey — where am I?"

They jabbered back at me in funny, squeaky voices. Like cartoon voices.

I couldn't understand them at all. It sounded like, "*Hubbahubbahubbahubba.*"

I could feel the panic sweeping over me. "Hey — answer me!" I shouted. "Where am I?"

"*Hubbahubbahubba.*"

I gripped the cage bars with both hands. "Do you think I'm some kind of *monkey*?" I shouted.

That's when I realized they weren't staring at me. They were staring *past* me.

I wasn't alone in the cage.

I heard heavy thuds pound the ground behind me.

I swung around — and stared at a huge creature with dark brown fur. At least four or five feet taller than me, and as wide as a Jeep! Lumbering forward on two fat, furry legs. Kicking up black clouds of dirt.

He gnashed two giant rows of teeth together as he thundered closer. His big black eyes were locked on mine.

An enormous APE. Like out of a horror movie.

King Kong versus Andy Meadows!

He kicked the beach ball against the cage bars and kept coming.

"I'm not a monkey!" I screamed. "I'm not a monkey!"

I was out of my head with fear. I didn't know *what* I was saying.

The big ape didn't seem to care. He tossed back his furry head and snarled. Then he gnashed his teeth together furiously.

He stopped for a moment. Picked up a disgusting blob of grass and weeds from the dirt. Shoved it into his big mouth and swallowed it whole.

Like he was showing me what he planned to do with me!

But apes don't eat meat — DO they?

Outside the cage, the crowd grew quiet. No one moved. No one blinked.

The snarling ape strode closer, kicking up a tornado of dirt.

"The tooth!" I cried out loud.

Yes. The tooth. My way out.

Why had I waited so long?

I grabbed for it. Wrapped my hand around it and lifted it from the front of my shirt.

But before I could make my escape wish, the ape reached out an enormous paw — and *swiped* it from me.

"Hey!" I made a frantic dive for it.

I bounced off his leg. Landed hard in the swirling dirt.

And watched the ape stomp away with the tooth.

17

The huge ape smacked the tire swing as he stomped past it. The tire rocked back and forth so hard, the whole tree shook.

"Give that tooth back!" I shouted.

The furry ape turned and raised the tooth in the air.

Was he going to toss it out of the cage?

I froze.

In my panic, I knew I had to get that tooth back. If I didn't, I could spend the *rest of my life* in this zoo cage.

The big ape held the tooth up close to his face, like he was studying it. He held the tooth out to me.

Then he pulled back his arm and *tossed* the tooth over the cage bars.

No. He only pretended to toss the tooth. He held it up to show me the tooth was still gripped tightly in his paw.

The creature was *teasing* me with it!

What could I do?

Fear paralyzed my brain. I couldn't think of anything.

A gust of wind blew through the cage. The beach ball bounced against my legs.

With a sigh, I started to kick it out of my way.

But then I stopped. I had an idea. I picked up the big ball in both hands.

Was the huge ape ready for a game of catch?

I raised the beach ball over my head — and heaved it at the ape.

The ape caught the ball in midair.

And the tooth fell from his hand to the ground.

I made a wild dive. Into the dirt. My hand scraped the ape's foot. My fingers wrapped around the leather cord.

Wet. The tooth had landed in a puddle of water.

I snatched the tooth up. Raised it to my face.

The ape leaned down — and made a wild grab for me with both paws.

I rolled out from under the big creature. Squeezed the wet tooth.

And screamed: "I wish I was back home safe and sound!"

ZZZZZZZAAAAAPPPPPPP!

A powerful current shocked my body. My arms shot up over my head. All my muscles tensed, then throbbed with pain.

Another electrical shock.

My teeth clamped together. I bit my tongue.

My throat closed. I couldn't breathe.

And still the current jolted through me, making me toss and spin and dance, a dance of pain and terror.

The last thing I saw were those big black ape eyes . . . gleaming black . . . staring at me in surprise.

The creature's eyes seemed to grow . . . to inflate to the size of black balloons.

And then, *everything* went black.

18

"Ohhhh." A sharp pain made the back of my head throb.

I tried to raise my head, but it felt as if it weighed a thousand pounds.

I opened my eyes. I saw a bright blur of yellow and white. Like a fried egg in front of my face.

I blinked until my eyes started to focus. I was gazing up at a high ceiling. The yellow yolk was a ceiling light.

"Where am I?" I groaned. My voice sounded hoarse, as if I'd been asleep for a long time.

I stretched my arms at my sides. I was sprawled on my back on a hard floor. I tried my legs. I pulled my knees up, sliding my shoes on the floor.

Yes. Legs and arms were working.

Faces appeared over me. Worried faces, squinting at me, studying me with tight-lipped frowns.

And then Marnie's face floated over me. "Andy? Are you waking up?"

"I don't know," I murmured. I rubbed the back of my head. "Am I awake? Where are we?"

Several people were kneeling at my sides. A white-haired woman was leaning over me, squeezing my wrist. Taking my pulse. A very pale man with thick eyeglasses helped pull me to a sitting position.

I leaned my head against a tile wall. In front of me, I saw a familiar store window. *Shoe Universe.*

"Did anyone call for an ambulance?" a man said. "Does he need an ambulance?"

"Did he faint?" a woman said. "Does he have a medical condition?"

"I don't think he needs an ambulance," the white-haired woman said. She let go of my wrist. Then she squinted at me. "Do you remember your name and address?"

"Yes," I said. "I'm Andy Meadows." I told her my address.

She climbed to her feet. "If you have a headache later, you should call your doctor."

"Okay," I said.

Shaking their heads and murmuring to each other, people started to leave.

Marnie dropped down beside me. "Andy, you got a nasty shock."

I stared hard at her. "Oh, my gosh! Marnie, how did you get here?" I cried.

She frowned at me. "Huh? What do you mean?"

"I — I totally forgot about you! I'm so sorry! I left you in that space capsule! I can't believe I did that! How did you get back to the mall from outer space?"

Her face went pale. "Uh-oh," she whispered. "Outer space?"

I nodded. Nodding made my head hurt.

"Maybe you DO need a doctor," Marnie said. "You're not making any sense."

She started to stand up. "I'll call your mom and dad. I'll tell them what happened. It won't take them long to get here."

"But, Marnie —" I grabbed her arm and pulled her back down beside me. "Remember? I was in bed? In a strange room. Not my own room. With people I'd never seen before. I made a wish. And we were in the space capsule. Then it began to fall to Earth. Then I was in a weird zoo. In a cage, like an animal. A huge ape came after me, and —"

Marnie pulled my hand off her arm. She jumped up. "Andy, don't move," she said. She pointed a trembling finger down at me. "Don't move."

"But, Marnie —"

"I'll get help," she said. She looked around frantically. "Listen. You're all mixed up. You've been here in the mall the whole time."

"Huh?" I gasped. "No way —"

"Andy, you got a shock, and it knocked you out. You've been out for almost ten minutes."

I gasped. "Huh? Only ten minutes?"

"Ten minutes," she said. "I was so worried —"

"But what about the space capsule?" I asked. "The ape in the zoo?"

Marnie squinted at me. "You haven't moved, Andy. You've been flat out on your back. You must have had weird dreams. From the shock."

My head was spinning. I felt totally confused.

Of course. Those adventures *had* to be dreams. My brain going berserk while I was out cold.

With a groan, I hoisted myself to my feet. I shook off my dizziness.

A few worried adults were still there watching me. I told them I felt fine. I watched them stroll away down the wide aisles.

I stretched my arms. "I feel a lot better," I told Marnie. "I feel —"

I stopped. My breath caught in my throat.

I stared hard. And then I let out a cry: "Marnie — why are YOU wearing my tooth?"

19

Marnie placed her hand over my forehead. After a few seconds, she said, "No. No fever."

I kept staring at the big tooth dangling from the cord around her neck. "My tooth —"

"*Your* tooth?" Marnie said. "Oh, wow. Since when is it *your* tooth?"

"But — but —" I sputtered.

"You're starting to scare me, Andy," she said. "I mean, really. I'm really worried about you. You hit your head on the hard floor when you fell. Maybe you have a concussion or something."

"I — I don't understand," I stammered.

"The tooth is mine," Marnie said. She squeezed it between two fingers. "It's never been yours."

"Not true!" I cried. "I bought it and —"

She raised a finger to my lips to hush me up.

"Don't you remember, Andy? At HorrorLand? We were in that little shop, and you didn't want the tooth. That weird shopkeeper offered it

78

to you first. And you said you thought it was dumb."

I shook my head. "Wait. That's not what I remember. I —"

"So I bought it from the shopkeeper. Chiller, or whatever his name was. I thought it was cool looking, so I bought it. It's *my* tooth. It's always been my tooth."

I felt dizzy again. The store windows tilted and swayed. The bright lights flickered above me.

I shut my eyes and waited for the dizziness to pass.

Is my memory totally messed up? I asked myself.

I thought I was the one who bought the tooth. Was that another one of my crazy dreams?

It didn't seem like a dream. Why did I remember so clearly that the wishing tooth belonged to *me*?

I had to get it straight in my mind. I hated feeling so totally confused.

I grabbed Marnie's shoulder. "Marnie, remember? A few days after we got back from HorrorLand? You were at my house, and my parents were talking about dinner. I had the tooth, and I made a wish that we would go *out* for dinner. Then, instantly, my dad said, 'Let's go out for dinner.' Remember?"

"Excuse me?" Marnie said. "Don't you remember? I made all the wishes, Andy. I wished that I could go with you? I wished your dad had a new car?"

"But — but —" I sputtered.

"Don't you remember? I wished to get twice as many French fries as you? And my wish came true?"

"Well . . . yes," I said. "Yes, I remember that. But —"

"And then I wished for a cow to appear in school so we'd get out for the day?"

"Yes. I remember that, too," I said.

"I made all the wishes," Marnie said, "because the tooth was mine. I was wearing it, Andy. So I made all those wishes."

I swallowed. I felt a shiver run down my back. "Do you think I'm going crazy?"

"I think the shock messed up your memory," Marnie said. "You had all those weird dreams while you were knocked out. And you imagined the tooth was yours."

"But it seems so real," I said. "Me wearing the tooth to school and to the mall and —"

"Andy, it's been in my dresser drawer since last Monday, the day I wished for the cow in school. You never owned the tooth. It's mine. Today is the first day I took it out of my drawer."

"Are you sure?" My voice came out high and tiny.

She nodded. "Don't you remember any of

this? I brought the tooth to the mall. And I started to make a wish in front of the shoe store. But I dropped the tooth. You tried to pick it up for me — remember? And then you got that terrible shock?"

I leaned against the wall. My brain was spinning in my head.

I felt sick. My stomach lurched.

I held my breath and pressed my hand over my mouth to keep from heaving.

Marnie went pale. "Are you okay? Are you feeling sick?"

"A . . . little," I choked out.

I couldn't stop my brain from churning.

How could my memory play such weird tricks on me?

The tooth belongs to Marnie?

Marnie bought the tooth necklace from Jonathan Chiller?

For a moment, I had the strangest feeling. *I'm still messed up!* I thought.

I'm confused because I'm in a dream.

I'm going to wake up and remember it all just the way it really happened.

But I knew that was wrong. I knew I was awake. No space capsule. No giant ape in a zoo cage.

No dream. Just the real world.

There was only one thing wrong. My brain was completely scrambled.

20

"How did it go at the mall?" Mom asked.

"Uh . . . not bad," I said.

I probably should have told the truth. But I wanted to go up to my room and think and be by myself. You know. Try to get my brain straight.

Mom and Dad were on the den floor with a Scrabble board spread out on the coffee table. They play the slowest, most boring Scrabble games. It's painful to play with them. They spend hours with their little dictionary, looking up words and then arguing about them.

And Mom always wins. I don't see the fun in it. But they love it.

I said good night and hurried away. I was halfway up the stairs. But Mom's voice stopped me. "Andy, let me see the sneakers you bought."

Sneakers?

Uh-oh.

"Uh . . . I didn't buy any," I said.

"You're kidding," Mom said. "Why not?"

"Just didn't see any I liked," I said. "Guess I'll have to go back."

"What *did* you buy there?" Dad called.

"Uh . . . well . . . nothing," I said. "You see, I got a very bad shock that knocked me out and made me have all these crazy dreams. And now my memory is totally messed up. And I'm freaking out because my brain is fried."

"That's nice," Dad said. "See you in the morning."

"Good night, dear," Mom added.

I *knew* they weren't listening!

I climbed the rest of the way to my room. I could hear them arguing down there. "*Fleg* is not a word," Mom said.

"Sure, it is," Dad said. "Look it up."

"No need. There's no such word as *fleg*. What is a fleg, anyway? Use it in a sentence."

"Okay. We fly the fleg on the Fourth of July."

They both broke up laughing. I closed my bedroom door. I wasn't in the mood for Dad's horrible Scrabble jokes.

My head felt like someone was pounding on it with a big wood mallet.

I decided to go to bed early.

When I wake up in the morning, the headache will be gone. And my memory will be back.

That's what I told myself.

I changed into my pajamas and climbed into bed. Then I pulled the covers up to my chin and shut my eyes.

It felt really good to be back in my own bed in my own room.

I settled my head deep into my pillow. I let out a long sigh and tried to relax.

But the sound outside my open window made me sit up with a jerk.

A long, low moan. Not a human sound.

And then another. Higher. Closer.

An animal howl. It rose and fell like an ambulance siren.

And then another. A dog's howl. An angry howl.

The Blue Kerlew Hound.

I knew it had to be that long-dead creature. The ghostly dog prowling right outside my house.

Howling . . . howling up at my window.

But — why?

I didn't have its tooth.

Why was it coming after *me*?

21

Another terrifying howl sent a chill down my back.

I jumped out of bed. I knew I wouldn't be able to sleep. I hurried to my window and peered down at the front yard.

No dog.

Pale moonlight made the yard look silvery, eerie. The flowers in my mom's flower bed swayed from side to side in a gusty breeze. A chipmunk scampered behind the big maple tree by the curb.

Was the ghostly dog *invisible*?

I hugged myself tightly, trying to stop my chills.

The next long howl made me jump. It seemed to be coming from right inside my room.

I spun around with a loud gasp.

No. *Calm down, Andy. Take a deep breath, dude.*

No way I could get to sleep. I clicked on my desk lamp and dropped down in front of my computer. I brought up Google and typed in *Blue Kerlew Hound.*

After a few seconds, the screen changed. I blinked. Only one entry came up. It had the headline: CREATURES OF LEGEND & MYTH.

I clicked on it. It took me to a weird Web site about Scotland. A long article filled the screen.

I scrolled down, searching for a picture. Something to show me what the hound looked like. But no. No picture or drawing.

I went back up to the top and began to read.

The whole story was there. The same story Jonathan Chiller told us in his shop at HorrorLand.

My eyes scanned down the screen, and I read the story all over again. The tiny town in the Highlands of Scotland . . . the mysterious blue dog . . . the bad luck it brought the town . . . the sorcerer who cursed the dog's teeth to drive it away . . . the sorcerer discovering the one tooth could grant wishes . . . the night the dog returned and the sorcerer was found torn to pieces.

It was all there. But then there was more.

My mouth dropped open as I read the bottom of the article. The part Jonathan Chiller didn't tell us . . . It said:

"The tooth has been missing for three hundred

years. No one knows if it is owned by anyone, or if it has disappeared for all time.

"Over time, the legend of the Kerlew Hound's tooth grew. It was said that the ghost dog roams the earth, looking for its missing tooth. And that each wish made with the tooth sends a signal. The hound follows the signals. And when the dog finally finds its tooth, the owner will share the same horrifying fate as the sorcerer."

My heart thundered in my chest as I read the last sentences:

"Of course, the story of the Blue Kerlew Hound is only legend, a tale made up in the Highlands of Scotland. But those people who know the legend admit they would not keep the tooth if they found it. No one wants to come face-to-face with the deadly hound."

It was late. Nearly one o'clock in the morning. But I didn't care.

I had to warn Marnie. I had to warn her that every wish she made on the tooth was dangerous.

I picked up my jeans from where I'd tossed them on the floor. I dug my cell phone out of the pocket and punched in Marnie's number. I listened to it ring . . . two times . . . three . . . four . . .

Finally, Marnie answered. "Andy? What do *you* want?" Her voice was hoarse.

"I know I woke you up," I said. "But this is important."

"It better be," she snapped. "What do you want?" She's a total grouch when you wake her up.

"Don't use the tooth anymore," I said. "Every wish is dangerous. No more wishes, Marnie. Every wish brings the blue hound closer."

Silence for a long moment.

Then Marnie burst out laughing.

"Nice try, Andy," she said. "Did you think that up all by yourself?"

"No. Really —" I said.

She laughed some more. "That's how jealous you are? You'd try a cheap trick like that to stop me from using my tooth?"

"Marnie, listen to me. You can look it up yourself. I'm not making it up —"

She groaned. "Andy, you tried to convince me we were in outer space — remember? Why should I believe a word you say?"

"It's true. It's really dangerous," I said. "Don't use the tooth, Marnie."

"Well, you just watch me tomorrow, Andy. Stand back and watch me — because I'm going to have some fun!"

22

I couldn't get to sleep for hours. When my alarm went off, I yawned and squinted out my bedroom window.

The sky was almost as dark as night, with storm clouds hanging low over the trees. I groaned and tried to sit up. I felt as if I had dark storm clouds fogging my brain.

At breakfast, Mom gave me a hard time about not buying sneakers. "I can't believe you wasted all that time yesterday, Andy. What did you do with the money I gave you?"

"I still have it," I said. "No problem. I was trying to be a good shopper."

"Good shopper?" Dad looked up from his laptop and laughed. "How can you be a good shopper if you don't buy anything?"

I wanted to tell them that I was serious about the electrical shock and everything. But then they would probably keep me out of school, ask

89

me a million questions, and make me go see Dr. Hanson.

I tilted the bowl to my mouth and slurped down the last drops of milk from my cornflakes. "I have to go," I said.

I rode my bike to school. I was half a block away when the rain started to come down. I tossed my bike at the bike rack and went running into the building.

I strode down the hall, shaking off water. My jacket was soaked through. And my hair was matted flat against my head.

I pulled open my locker. Marnie came running up. "Andy, you feeling okay?" she asked.

She didn't give me a chance to answer. She swung herself around. "Check out the new backpack. It's Prada. Feel the leather."

I felt the leather. "Smooth," I said. "Doesn't that cost, like, a thousand dollars or something?"

Her green eyes flashed. "I didn't pay for it. I *wished* for it."

Then I saw the big tooth dangling on its cord around her neck.

"These new jeans, too," Marnie said. "I never had straight-leg jeans that fit this well." She wrapped her fingers around the tooth. "Think I'm going to wish for another pair."

She turned and started down the hall. I chased after her. "Listen, Marnie, I Googled the whole thing last night," I said. "The tooth is more dangerous than Jonathan Chiller told us."

Marnie rolled her eyes. "We've been there, Andy," she said. "Remember? You called me last night? I didn't believe you then. Why should I believe you now?"

"Because it's true?" I said.

She waved to a friend. "Got to go, dude."

"I — I heard the dog again last night," I said. "Every wish brings it closer."

"If the big blue dog comes after me, I'll wish it away!" Marnie said. Then she ran to catch up to her friend. I watched her showing off her new backpack.

The hall was noisy with kids shouting and laughing and locker doors slamming. But in my mind, I kept hearing the eerie howls, the mournful cries that had kept me up most of the night.

I half slept through class all morning. Luckily, Mrs. Parker didn't call on me.

When the bell rang for our mid-morning break, Marnie came running up to me with a big grin. She waved a paper in front of my face. "Andy, check it out."

I grabbed it and studied it. "Your math quiz? You got an A?"

Marnie is a total moron in math.

She nodded, giggling.

I stared at her. "You . . . you *wished* it?"

"Andy, I'm never going to get a bad grade in math again!" She raised the tooth to her mouth and kissed it. "I'm a genius now. I'm a math genius!"

"Nice," I said. My stomach suddenly felt as if I'd swallowed a big rock. "How many wishes are you going to make today?"

She grinned. "Maybe a million." She gave me a punch in the stomach and hurried away.

I stood there, thinking hard. What if the story I read last night was true? What if every wish Marnie made brought the ghost hound closer?

I felt totally tense. Every muscle in my body had a knot in it.

Worst of all, my memory still wasn't working. I didn't remember anything correctly that happened before the electrical shock.

I jumped when I felt a hand on my shoulder. I turned to see Mrs. Parker gazing down at me.

Mrs. Parker is about six feet tall and very thin. She has blond hair and blue eyes. She looks like a model in some of the magazines my mom reads. She told us she comes from Norway, where just about everyone looks like her.

Now all of us guys want to move to Norway!

"Andy, what are you thinking about so intensely?" she asked.

"Uh . . . math," I said.

She laughed. She has a funny little laugh that sounds like a canary chirping. "Why don't I believe you?"

"Because I'm lying?"

That made her chirp even harder. "We're having a very interesting assembly this afternoon," she told me. "Congressman Boltz is going to tell us some fascinating things that have happened to him in Washington."

Oh, thrills, I thought. *Maybe if I sit in a back row, I can catch up on my sleep.*

"And he's going to announce the winner of the five-hundred-dollar essay prize."

That woke me up. "I could win that," I said. "I worked really hard on that essay."

"Yes, you did," Mrs. Parker said. "I thought yours was the best, Andy. The best — by far. But I wasn't one of the judges."

I flashed her a smile. "Now I really *am* thinking of math," I said. "I'm thinking about the number five hundred!"

The bell rang. "Good luck," Mrs. Parker said. She headed to her desk to get ready for class.

All through class, I kept thinking about the five hundred dollars. Thinking about how Mrs. Parker said my essay was the best. By far.

So . . . how big a loser am I?

The biggest loser in school — by far?

Why did I even *think* I had a chance?

I stayed awake all through Congressman Boltz's talk in the auditorium. He had some pretty funny stories about going to the wrong meetings and getting locked in his office one night.

He was younger than I thought he'd be. Actually, he was a pretty cool guy.

And then it came time to announce the big prize winner in the essay contest. I sat up straight in my seat and gripped the chair arms. I held my breath.

A hush fell over the auditorium. A lot of kids had entered the essay contest. A lot of kids believed they had a chance of winning.

Jerks. All of us.

Because, of course, Congressman Boltz leaned into the microphone and announced: "The grand prize winner is sixth-grader . . . Marnie Myers!"

Some kids cheered as Marnie jumped up. She acted totally surprised. She screamed and jumped up and down and tore at her hair and even had tears in her eyes.

I just groaned and slumped down in my seat as low as I could go.

I covered my face in my hands. I didn't want to watch her go onstage and collect the big check.

I never had a chance.

*   *   *

School ended after the assembly. Some kids wanted to hang around the playground and get up a soccer game. But I told them I had to hurry home.

I didn't feel like talking to anyone.

I saw Marnie joining the game. I knew she'd suddenly be the best soccer player in school history.

Another wish . . . and another wish . . . and another wish. When I shut my eyes, I could picture the snarling blue hound ripping us both apart . . . tearing off our arms and legs . . . snapping and frothing, chewing . . . chewing . . . until we were just scraps of meat.

All because Marnie wouldn't stop wishing.

I slumped home, kicking stones and things out of my way.

Mom and Dad were at work. I was glad. I didn't want to talk to them, either. Face it. I was in a very bad mood.

I didn't know it. I was about to get in an even *worse* mood.

I pulled myself up to my bedroom. I was hot and sweaty from the walk home so I tugged off my T-shirt. And grabbed a fresh one from the dresser drawer.

But before I pulled it on, I caught a glimpse of myself in the dresser mirror.

And I let out a scream of total shock.

23

I leaned over the dresser and brought my face up close to the mirror.

I was breathing hard, my chest thumping. My breath steamed the glass.

It *had* to be a shadow I'd seen. That dark line across my neck.

I raised my fingers to it.

No. Not a shadow. It was real.

A cut in my neck. A dark red line. "A bruise," I whispered to myself.

I grabbed the top of the dresser with both hands. And turned my face one way, then the other.

Yes, that thin line was a bruise. The bruise made when Marnie tried to tug the tooth cord off me. In front of the shoe store.

She tried to take it away from me. I remembered so clearly. She pulled so hard, the leather dug into my neck.

The bruise was still there.

"Marnie LIED!" I screamed. "Marnie LIED!"

I stood there screaming at my reflection in the dresser mirror.

She wanted the tooth so badly.

She said she would do ANYTHING to have the tooth.

So when I got that shock . . . when I blacked out . . . when I was out cold . . . she TOOK it.

She put the tooth around her neck. And when I woke up, she made me think I was crazy. She made me think my memory was messed up. She really made me believe that the tooth had been hers the whole time.

Wow.

I stared into the mirror at the bruise on my neck.

Wow. Wow. Wow.

I *knew* Marnie wanted the tooth badly. But I didn't know HOW badly.

Bad enough to make her own cousin think he was losing his mind!

And now, here she was, making wish after wish after wish. Acing every quiz and test, winning big bucks in the essay contest. Getting everything she wanted.

With MY tooth!

Mine! Mine!

I couldn't help it. My anger boiled over. I felt like my head exploded.

I totally lost it.

I started pounding the dresser with both fists. Pounding it. Punching it. As if it were Marnie.

Punching the dresser again and again. Punching till my fists throbbed.

I stopped when I saw my mom's reflection in the mirror. Her eyes were bulging and her mouth hung wide open.

Panting hard, my fists aching, I slowly turned to face her.

"Andy?" she asked, staring hard at me. "Andy? Are you okay?"

"No. I'm *not* okay," I gasped. "I have to murder my cousin. I have no choice, Mom. I'm really sorry — but I have to murder my cousin Marnie."

"Go ahead. That's no problem," Mom said. "I don't like her, either."

24

That didn't really happen.

I didn't say that, and Mom sure didn't say that, either.

I was so angry, so out-of-control, that's what I *wished* we had said.

But, back up. It really went like this:

MOM: "Andy? What are you doing? Are you okay?"

ME: "Uh, yeah, Mom. One of the dresser drawers stuck. That's all."

She didn't move. Just stood there staring at me. "Are you sure?"

"Yeah. I'm fine, Mom. Really."

I could see that she didn't believe me. But she finally turned and started for the hall. "Don't beat up your furniture, Andy," she said from the doorway.

"No, Mom," I said softly. "I'll try to give the dresser a break."

She headed downstairs to make dinner.

I let out a long sigh. My fists ached from pounding my poor dresser.

I knew who I *really* wanted to pound.

I kept picturing Marnie, leaning over me at the mall. Acting so worried after I'd been knocked out. Asking me if I was okay — with *my tooth* dangling around her neck.

I sat down in my desk chair. My head spun with plan after plan for revenge.

I saw myself grabbing the tooth away from Marnie. Then I'd wish that she would turn into a chicken. And there she'd be, all brown and yellow feathers, clucking away, pecking the floor for seed.

Then maybe after a few weeks, I'd decide to give her a break and change her back.

That made me laugh.

I imagined changing Marnie into all kinds of animals. Maybe a big, fat cow. Then she could stampede through the school, and we'd all get the day off again!

Not bad.

But I knew I could do better. If I thought about it long enough, I knew I could plan the perfect revenge.

I was still plotting and scheming later that night as I climbed into bed — and heard the animal howl outside my window. The revenge plots leaped from my mind. I sat up straight and listened.

Another howl rose from beneath my window. So close. It could be coming from my *room*!

That thought sent a cold shiver down my whole body.

Did anyone else hear it?

Once again, I tiptoed to the window. I pulled it open all the way. A cool gust of wind brushed my pajamas.

The dog howled again.

Could it be the Blue Kerlew? Was it back for its tooth?

I gripped the ledge and leaned out the window. I stared down into total darkness. I couldn't even see the flower bed at the side of the house.

Another frightening howl.

And then I saw it. I SAW it!

And in that instant, I knew what my revenge against Marnie was going to be. I knew *the dog* would bring me my revenge!

25

A few days later, I hurried up to Marnie in the lunchroom at school. "Marnie, I can't sleep at night because that creepy dog keeps howling outside my window," I said. "Could you use your tooth for me? Make a wish that the dog would go away?"

She scrunched up her face. "I'm kind of busy . . ."

"Well, could you maybe help me with something else?" I asked.

She waved to some girls at a table across the lunchroom. She wasn't even listening to me.

"I'm building a game-arcade machine for my class project," I said. "It's going to be awesome. Just like the game machines they have in arcades."

She squinted at me. "So?"

"I downloaded a ton of old video games. And I have a monitor to use. But I'm having trouble building the box for it. Could you make a wish that I get it done in time?"

"I don't think so," Marnie said. "That really wouldn't be fair to the other kids — would it?"

"But —"

She waved me off and hurried to join her friends.

I almost tossed my lunch tray at her. That really was the last straw.

Saturday afternoon, I called Marnie. "Can you come over?" I asked.

"I don't know," she said. She sounded out of breath. "I just won a tennis tournament. You know. At the indoor courts. It was a long match. It took five sets. I let the other girl win a couple sets. You know. To make it look good."

"Wow," I said. "You really are enjoying that wishing tooth, aren't you! I guess you're glad you bought it."

"Hel-lo," Marnie said. "It's the *best* thing I ever bought. Too bad that guy Chiller didn't have one for you, Andy."

I balled my hands into tight fists. I wanted to growl like an animal into the phone.

Instead, I said, "Yeah. Too bad. Listen, Marnie, I need help with my game machine. The one I told you about? Can you come over? All of my friends are busy."

"What do you want me to do?" she asked.

"I'm building the frame for it. And I can't do it by myself."

"If we finish it, can we play it?" Marnie asked.

"Yeah. Sure," I said. "I downloaded all the great old games. *Ms. Pac-Man* . . . *Frogger* . . . *Space Invaders* . . . "

"Cool."

I knew what she wanted to do. She wanted to come over, play my game machine — and beat me at all the games.

Is there a more competitive person in the world than Marnie?

I don't think so.

Without thinking, I was rubbing the slender bruise on my neck. "So, can you come over and help me?"

"Yeah, I guess. I'm probably better at building that thing than you. See you after lunch."

Two hours later, Marnie and I were working in my garage.

First, she had to show off the cool new leather jacket she had wished for and received for free.

The tooth was around her neck, under her T-shirt. I could see the leather cord.

Everyone in sixth grade has to build some kind of machine. Last week, I downloaded the video games onto my dad's old computer. Now the plan was to build a wooden case around the computer to make it look like an arcade game.

Dad and I bought the lumber we needed. We painted it all bright red and yellow. And Dad helped me saw it into the right shapes.

Now I just had to fasten the sides and back together. Fit the computer inside so the monitor screen showed in the front. Set up the control pads. And nail on a bottom.

I had the plans all drawn out. It wasn't hard. It just took two people.

Marnie and I carefully fit one of the red side panels to the back. I had a jar of nails ready. I poured some of them onto the garage floor and picked up a hammer.

"Just hold the two boards like this," I said. "And I'll pound in a few nails."

Marnie pressed the side and back boards together. "Where does the power cord go?" she asked.

I pointed. "See that hole in the back panel? It'll fit through there."

"And what about ventilation?" Marnie asked. "Did you leave room for a fan or anything?"

What a know-it-all! Did she *always* have to show off?

"It won't get too hot," I said. "I left plenty of air space around the computer."

"This is awesome," Marnie said. "If it works."

"It'll work," I said. I pounded the first nail. It went in a little crooked. But it went in.

"I can pound straighter than that," Marnie said. "Here. Give me the hammer. I'll do it."

Before I could answer, I heard a sound.

A dog's howl.

"Hey!" I let out a cry. I jumped — and kicked over the jar of nails.

The dog's howl rose high and shrill, then dropped. It sounded so close — like it was in the driveway.

I turned to Marnie. "D-did you hear that?" I stammered.

She didn't have to answer. I saw the look of fear on her face.

"Is that the dog you heard before?" she asked.

I nodded. "I . . . think so."

The dog howled again. The sound echoed off the concrete garage walls.

Marnie dropped the two boards. They clattered onto the floor in front of her. She took a step back.

"It sounds . . . ghostly," she whispered. "Close and far away at the same time. Not like a real dog."

The next howl was even closer. And then I saw the creature's shadow slide over the driveway by the garage door.

"Look out." My voice shook. "Here it comes."

26

Marnie's eyes grew wide. She took another step back — and stumbled into my dad's power mower.

"Ow!" She tumbled into the garage wall, and a garden rake fell off its hook and crashed to the concrete floor.

I kicked it out of the way. Then I backed up beside Marnie.

We both watched as the shadow lengthened over the driveway.

A dark head slid into view.

Marnie gasped.

The big front paws moved silently over the ground. The dog lowered its head as it stepped into its own shadow.

"A hound dog!" I whispered to Marnie. I started to tremble.

She swallowed. Tried to speak. But no sound came out.

The dog lumbered into the shade of the garage.

Its big dark eyes were wet as it turned its gaze on us. Its long, ragged ears drooped down. Its tongue hung loosely out of one side of its gaping mouth.

"It's . . . so big!" Marnie murmured, finally finding her voice.

The dog uttered a low growl.

I gasped. "Marnie — look at its fur! It's . . . BLUE!"

"It . . . it *can't* be!" she cried. She shuddered. Her teeth were chattering.

"The B-blue Kerlew Hound," I stammered.

Growling softly, it moved toward us, head lowered, wet eyes in a dead stare.

"It's messed up," Marnie whispered. "Its fur is all matted and filthy. It's got all that dirt stuck to it."

"Leaves," I said. "Sticks and mud and leaves." I gasped. "Like it came from a *graveyard*!"

"Nooooo!" Marnie uttered a frightened cry. I could see her legs trembling. She pressed her back against the garage wall.

The dog's tail stood straight out. The frightening creature made a snuffling sound as it moved closer. One slow step at a time.

"Maybe we can make a run for it," I whispered. I motioned toward the garage door.

"I . . . don't think so," Marnie stammered. "It's so big. How could we get around it? It . . . it's not a real dog — right? It's . . . back from the dead."

I nodded, huddling close to my cousin. "It's the Blue Kerlew Hound. It's here. And you know what it came for. It came to take back its tooth!"

Marnie grabbed my hand. Her hand was cold as ice. "Andy," she whispered, "it looks so angry. What is it going to *do* to us?"

27

The big dog took another lumbering step toward us. It hunkered in the middle of the garage now, blocking our way to the door.

"We can call for help," Marnie whispered. "If we shout, your parents —"

"They're not home," I said.

She uttered another cry. Her chin was trembling. She had her arms crossed tightly in front of her, like a shield.

I stared down at the dirt and dead leaves clinging to the creature's blue fur.

I took a step forward. I lowered my head toward it.

"Don't look at me," I said to the dog. I pointed to Marnie. "It's HER tooth!"

"Andy — what are you *doing*?" Marnie cried.

I ignored her and talked to the hound. "It's Marnie's tooth. She bought it. She bought it in HorrorLand, and she's been wearing it ever since."

The dog raised its wet eyes to Marnie and uttered a low, menacing growl.

"Give it to him, Marnie!" I shouted. "Quick! Give him the tooth! Or else he'll tear you to pieces! Like the sorcerer!"

"Noooo!" Marnie wailed.

She tugged at the tooth. She struggled to pull the cord off her neck.

The cord caught in her hair. Finally, she jerked it loose. Then she jammed the tooth into my hand.

"It's *Andy's*!" she cried to the dog. "It's not mine! It's his! I — I stole it from him!"

The old hound gazed up at her without moving.

"I stole it from him!" Marnie wailed. "Andy is the one who bought it. It's his. REALLY!"

A heavy silence fell over the garage.

And then, I couldn't hold it in any longer. I burst out laughing.

"I KNEW it!" I cried. "I *knew* you were a thief, Marnie!"

Her mouth dropped open. Her eyes bulged. "Andy? Why are you laughing? Th-that dog —"

"You're busted, Marnie," I said. I slapped her on the back. "I totally *got* you! That dog isn't the Blue Kerlew Hound. That's Jack, my new neighbor's dog."

Marnie stared at the dog. "You — you planned this? You did this to scare me?"

I nodded. "To scare the truth out of you," I said.

She shook her head. "Well . . . you really got me," she admitted. "I was a little scared."

"A *little* scared?" I laughed again. I was totally enjoying myself.

Talk about a plan working perfectly!

She motioned with her head. "That dog — ?"

"It's the dog that's been keeping me up for nights," I said. "At first I thought it was the Blue Kerlew Hound. But then I realized it was my new neighbor's dog, Jack. Jack isn't used to this neighborhood. So he howls at night.

"I went to see the new neighbor," I continued. "Mr. Murphy. He said he was sorry about the hound dog howling every night. But when I saw the dog, it gave me the idea."

"To scare me?" Marnie said.

"To spray it blue and scare you," I said. "And to get you to admit you stole my wishing tooth."

Marnie's cheeks turned bright red. "I admit it," she said in a whisper. "Okay? Happy? I admit it."

I laughed. "You're totally blushing. You're actually embarrassed, aren't you!"

She lowered her eyes. "Yes. I'm embarrassed. It was crazy. Stealing that tooth necklace while you were out cold. Then saying it was mine all along."

She sighed. "I think I lost my mind. I'm sorry, Andy. Really. You must hate me. I'm so sorry."

I had to laugh again. I was so pleased with myself.

I started over to Jack. "Good boy," I said. But then I stopped.

The blue hound took a step closer. The creature made a snuffling sound. Slowly, slowly, it raised its head. And . . .

And . . .

And . . . a shock of *horror* made my whole body jerk.

"Hey!" I cried. "Hey! Wait! What's going *on* here? That's the WRONG DOG!"

28

"Wrong dog?" Marnie cried. "Andy, what are you *talking* about?"

My breath caught in my throat. I couldn't move. Couldn't *speak*!

I kept my eyes on the growling hound.

Not Jack. Definitely not Jack.

I knew what I was staring at. But how could it be? How could I be staring at the *real* Blue Kerlew Hound?

"I — I borrowed Mr. Murphy's hound dog," I stammered. "I sprayed him blue. I stuck twigs and mud on him. But . . . but . . ."

Suddenly, another dog slunk into view at the garage door. Smaller. Cleaner. It was Jack. Looking forlorn. His head down. His whole body quivering.

"Who's that other dog?" Marnie pointed.

"Th-that's Jack," I said, my voice trembling. "That's the dog I borrowed. He's too frightened to come in. Look. He's totally scared . . . scared of the Blue Kerlew Hound. He knows this dog is evil."

Jack whimpered and hurried out of sight.

The Blue Kerlew Hound bared its ugly jagged teeth and snarled at us.

"This — this is all your fault," Marnie stammered.

"MY fault?" I cried. "YOU'RE the one who kept making all the wishes. I warned you that each wish brought the hound closer. But you didn't believe me."

Marnie didn't reply.

White froth bubbled out of the evil dog's open mouth. It lowered its head, preparing to attack.

I pressed my back against the garage wall.

Marnie shuddered again. "What are we going to do?"

I stared down at the dirt and dead leaves clinging to the creature's blue fur. From the graveyard . . . From the grave . . .

The dog tensed its back, preparing to leap at us.

"Give it to him, Marnie!" I shouted. "Quick! Give him the tooth! That's what he came for! Give him the tooth — or else he'll tear us to pieces!"

"Andy — YOU have it!" she cried. "The tooth — you're squeezing it in your hand!"

I was so terrified, I didn't even feel it.

An ugly roar escaped the dog's throat. He turned on me. His dark eyes suddenly glowed bright RED!

He bent his back legs, preparing to leap.

I squeezed the tooth in my hand. And shouted at the top of my lungs. "I WISH FOR THE HOUND TO DISAPPEAR!"

Nothing happened.

I squeezed the tooth so hard, it dug into my palm. I held my breath and stared at the growling beast.

I shouted the wish again. "I wish for the hound to disappear!"

Nothing happened.

The evil hound stared up at us.

The wishes made on his tooth didn't work on him.

The dog reared back — kicked off from the garage floor — and attacked.

It leaped onto me, snarling and growling. I felt its putrid breath on my face. Then I felt its heavy paws wrap around my waist. So powerful. The dog heaved its weight against me — and I slammed hard against the wall.

I couldn't move. It had me pinned against the concrete. White slobber poured from its mouth as it opened its jaws — and slashed its deadly teeth at my face.

29

I struggled to break free. But the huge hound had me trapped. It pressed its enormous paws down on me.

The dog smelled like rotting meat. I could feel its hot drool as its gaping mouth prepared to close — to clamp its powerful fangs down on me.

I still had the tooth wrapped in my hand.

If I can't make HIM disappear, I thought, *maybe I can make US disappear!* "I — I wish Marnie and I were *invisible*!" I choked out.

Would *this* wish work?

Yes!

I knew the wish had been granted when the hound let out a yelp of surprise.

The dog dropped to the floor. His red eyes swept rapidly from right to left, searching for us.

I turned. I couldn't see Marnie beside me.

We were both invisible!

"Run!" I screamed. "To the house! He can't see us!"

The dog uttered a puzzled whine.

I took off, running hard.

I hoped Marnie was running beside me.

My heart pounded as I ran full speed down the driveway to the kitchen door.

Would we be safe inside the house?

I glanced back. The dog had started trotting toward the house. Did he figure out where we were? Could he hear us?

Gasping for breath, I leaped onto the back stoop.

Got to get inside . . . Got to get inside . . .

I grasped the handle to the back door, and —

— and my hand went right through it.

"Huh?"

I grabbed for the door handle again. No. I couldn't feel it. My fingers went right through it.

I grabbed at it again. Again.

I couldn't touch anything. I couldn't *move* anything! This is not what I thought would happen if you were invisible.

"Andy — hurry!" Marnie cried, right behind me on the stoop. "The dog smells us. He's coming for us! Hurry! Open the door!"

"I — I can't!" I cried. "My hand is going right through the handle! We're trapped out here! We can't get inside!"

"Look out!" Marnie screamed. "Here he COMES!"

30

Sniffing the air, the hound came running toward the back stoop.

I didn't think. I just moved.

I leaned my shoulder against the kitchen door and pushed.

And I slipped right through the wooden door. Startled, I stumbled halfway across the kitchen.

"Marnie!" I screamed at the top of my lungs. "Go through the door! You can dive right through the door!"

"Why are you screaming?" she said. "I'm standing right next to you."

I took in a deep, shuddering breath. My heart pounded so hard, I felt dizzy. I tried to lean against the kitchen counter. But I couldn't feel it. I sank halfway through it.

"Did you hear that growl?" Marnie asked, close beside me. I didn't have to see her to know how terrified she was. "It's out there, Andy. And it knows we're in here."

A terrifying thought made me feel even diz-zier. "Do you think the hound can go through a solid door, too?"

"M-maybe," Marni stammered. "It's a ghost, right? It can probably go through anything."

"What are we going to do?" I asked, my voice no stronger than a whisper.

Silence.

We were both thinking hard.

From the backyard, I heard another low, men-acing growl.

I crossed the kitchen to the back window and peered out. The blue hound sat in the driveway, sniffing the air.

"It's waiting for us to come out," I said. "We're trapped in here."

"Maybe we can call for help," Marnie said from the kitchen counter. "Call your parents. Or my parents. Maybe if someone else comes, the dog won't want to show itself..."

"...and it will run away." I finished her thought for her. "Maybe," I said. "It's a plan, I guess."

Outside, the dog let out a long angry howl.

I stepped up to the wall phone next to the kitchen table. "My dad has his cell," I said. "I'll try him first."

I reached for the phone. "Oh, nooooo," I moaned.

I grabbed at it again. "No. This isn't happening."

"You can't pick it up?" Marnie asked.

"My hand goes right through it," I said. "How could I forget? This is so weird. We can't touch or pick up anything. No way we can call for help."

"Well, then make us visible again so we can call for help," Marnie said. "Hurry — before that dog gets restless and comes charging in here."

"Yes. I'll make a wish," I said. "The tooth. I —"

A wave of panic rolled over me. I couldn't breathe. I couldn't see straight!

"Andy — what's wrong?" Marnie asked.

"The tooth," I choked out. "I don't have it. It must have fallen from my hand when I turned invisible."

A long silence. Then Marnie whispered, "You really don't have it?"

"It — it must have fallen to the garage floor," I said. "It's . . . in the garage!"

"Well, you have to go get it!" Marnie screamed. "Go! Hurry!"

"Me?" I cried. "Why do I have to do it?"

"It's your tooth!" Marnie cried.

"HA!" I exclaimed. "Nice how you remember whose tooth it is when you want me to risk my LIFE!"

"I'm sorry," Marnie said. "Sorry I acted like such a jerk. But you have to go get the tooth, Andy. If you don't, we'll be invisible *forever*!"

I took a few trembling steps to the kitchen door. *The hound can't see me,* I told myself. *But I have to walk right past him to get into the garage.*

"Just run," Marnie said. "Run right past him. You can do it, Andy. You *have* to!"

My legs were shaking so hard, I could barely walk. I took another deep breath.

And pushed myself through the kitchen door. Onto the back stoop.

As soon as I burst outside, the dog raised its head. It climbed to its feet.

Alert. Suddenly very alert. It opened its jaws in a fierce growl.

Then it lowered its head menacingly. And came trotting toward me, growling all the way.

31

It can't see me.

The dog can't see me.

I kept repeating those words to myself over and over.

I stepped off the stoop. Moving silently, carefully, I made my way across the grass toward the garage.

Don't make a sound, I told myself.

Don't make a sound. The dog can't see you.

The dog stopped suddenly. It was only a few feet from me now.

I could smell it. Smell the sour aroma of the graveyard on its fur.

And I knew it could smell me, too.

It raised its head. Sniffed the air again. And STARED RIGHT AT ME.

It can't see me. It can't see me.

I took off running. I lowered my head and shoulders and rocketed toward the garage.

My invisible sneakers didn't make a sound as I stormed up the driveway. Into the shadows of the garage.

I glanced back.

The dog had turned. Its head was lowered again, and it was trotting in my direction.

I let out a gasp. Was I going to be trapped in the garage with the evil hound?

Squinting into the dim light of the garage, I saw the tooth. On the concrete floor.

I dove for it.

I could hear the dog pick up its steps behind me. It knew where I was.

I grabbed the tooth.

My hand went right through it.

"Oh, noooo."

I tried to pinch it between my thumb and pointer finger. But I couldn't touch it. I couldn't pick up the tooth.

I heard a raging snarl. The dog thundered into the garage.

It bared its long fangs. White drool dripped from his mouth. The hound knew it had me . . . had me trapped.

32

My legs were shaking too hard to hold me. I dropped to my knees.

My knee landed on the tooth. I couldn't feel it. But maybe if I was covering it . . . maybe . . .

"I wish Marnie and I were visible again!" I screamed.

Startled by my cry, the hound stopped.

And, yes! *Yes!* There I was! I saw my legs . . . my knees. I saw my arms. I shook my hands rapidly in the air.

I was back.

Back in time to be torn to pieces by the furious ghost dog!

"No!" I cried.

I picked up the tooth. I jumped to my feet. "I know why you came back!" I told it. "You came back for this."

I waved the tooth in front of me.

"The sorcerer didn't return it," I said. "And so

you tore him apart. But I'm going to return it. I'm giving you back your tooth!"

I pulled my arm back — and heaved the tooth as hard as I could.

I watched it sail out of the garage . . . over the driveway. The tooth and its cord flew to the front, nearly to the street.

"Go get it!" I shouted to the dog. "It's all yours!"

With a final growl, the dog spun away from me. It lowered its head and raced down the driveway to get its prize.

I hunched over with my hands on my knees and struggled to catch my breath. When I looked up, I saw Marnie poke her head out the kitchen door.

"Is it gone?" she called. "Andy, we're visible again! Did you wish that dog away? Is it really gone?"

I nodded. "I . . . gave it back the tooth," I choked out.

I gazed down the driveway. I didn't see the hound. "I think it's gone," I said. "I think it's gone for good!"

Marnie and I both cheered. Marnie hurried over to me. We cheered again, did a victory dance, and touched knuckles.

Then I gasped. A blue dog walked out slowly from the side of the garage.

It took me a few seconds to remember it was Jack. Poor, frightened Jack.

I started over to him. "It's okay, Jack. That bad dog is gone," I said.

I heard a shout. I turned and saw a man jogging up the driveway.

"Mr. Murphy!" I called. "You're back!"

He trotted up to Marnie and me. "How's it going?" he asked. "How is my buddy Jack?"

I pointed. "He's right there. Thanks for letting him visit," I said.

Mr. Murphy took a few steps toward the hound. Then he stopped.

His mouth dropped open. He turned to me.

"What's wrong?" I asked.

"I'll *tell* you what's wrong," he said. "This isn't my dog!"

33

A shock of fear made my heart skip a beat.

"Oh, no!" I gasped. Did the *wrong dog* run away?

Is the evil ghost dog standing here?

"This *can't* be my dog!" Mr. Murphy laughed. "My dog is brown," he said. "This dog is BLUE!"

He wrapped his arms around the dog's neck. It licked his face.

I let out a long sigh of relief. Mr. Murphy was joking. The dog was Jack after all.

"I — I can explain," I stammered.

"We were making a video for school," Marnie chimed in. "About a weird dog."

"I sprayed him blue, Mr. Murphy," I said. "It will come right out. Marnie and I will give him a bath. Then we'll bring him home to you."

Mr. Murphy scratched his head. "You turned Jack blue? What kind of video were you making?" he asked. "A *horror* video?"

"Uh . . . yes," I said. "A very realistic horror video."

Marnie and I pulled a big metal tub from the garage. We plopped Jack inside it with lots of sudsy water. I used the garden hose to spray the blue color off his fur.

Marnie said good-bye and headed for home. I dried Jack off and returned him to Mr. Murphy.

I walked home with a big smile on my face. Now life would return to normal. I decided I *love* normal!

Late that night, I lay in bed, still awake. I guess it was hard to calm down after such a terrifying day.

I was just closing my eyes when I heard the first dog howl.

I sat straight up in bed. A gasp escaped my throat.

Another long howl. So nearby. Like right outside my window.

I scolded myself for getting scared. That had to be Jack. Jack across the street, up to his old tricks.

I heard another low howl.

And then my phone rang.

So late at night?

I clicked it on. "Hello? Marnie?" I said. "What's up? What's the problem?"

130

"Well . . ." She hesitated. "Andy, I have a confession to make," she said.

Outside, the dog howls sounded angry.

"Confession?" I asked. I pressed the phone to my ear. "Marnie, what are you talking about?"

"I . . . uh . . . I found the tooth in the driveway," Marnie said. "Don't kill me, okay?"

"You *what*? I cried.

"I found the tooth," Marnie said. "I . . . couldn't resist it. I took it back."

I swallowed. I suddenly felt very cold. "You mean the Blue Kerlew Hound didn't get its tooth?" I said in a weak cry.

"I guess not," Marnie said. "I'm wearing the tooth. But I promise I'll share, Andy. This time, I'll share."

EPILOGUE

34

How could I sleep? I sat straight up in bed, listening to the dog howl outside. The clock said it was two in the morning. But I was wide-awake.

Suddenly, I saw a bright green-yellow glow on the wall in front of me. It was coming from the top of my bookshelf.

"Huh?" Was I dreaming again? Going crazy?

Blinking into the shimmering light, I made my way across the room.

I stared at the little Horror. The toy Horror that the shopkeeper at HorrorLand had attached to my souvenir package. The green-yellow glow flared all around it.

I remembered what the old guy said. Jonathan Chiller. I remember he put the tooth in a box. And wrapped the box in ribbon. And attached the little Horror to the ribbon.

And then he said, "Take a little Horror home with you."

And now the Horror was suddenly glowing on my bookshelf. Glowing like a candle.

I couldn't take my eyes off it. I was drawn to it. Pulled . . .

Pulled into its gleaming light.

Surrounded by the shimmering green-yellow flames. They swept around me. Lifting me from my room. Pulling me . . . pulling me into their strange fire.

"No!" I uttered a cry. I realized instantly I was no longer at home.

My eyes adjusted to the light, and I saw shelf after shelf of weird objects, gifts and souvenirs.

I was back in the little shop. Back in Chiller House.

And Jonathan Chiller stood in front of me with a grin on his face. Not a friendly grin. It was somehow cold and menacing.

"H-how did I get back here?" I choked out.

He didn't answer my question. Instead, he pushed the little square spectacles back on his pointed nose. Then he said, "Welcome back, Andy."

"But — why?" I cried. "Why am I here?"

"It's payback time," Chiller replied in his croaky old man voice. "Time to pay for your gift."

"Excuse me?"

"Time for you to pay me back for all the fun you've had with your wishing tooth."

"But — but —" I sputtered. "I didn't *have* any fun!"

Chiller's smile tightened against his pale face. "Don't worry, Andy," he whispered. "The fun is just *beginning*! MY kind of fun!"

HorrorLand

TRADING CARDS

MURDER THE CLOWN

REAL NAME: Murder the Dentist
BORN: Yes
HOMETOWN: New Yuck City
SCHOOL: All-Breed Doggie Obedience School
PROUDEST ACHIEVEMENT:
Invented the Squirting Electric Chair

HORRORLAND SPLAT STATS

HEAD SIZE:
NOSE HAIR LENGTH:
LACK OF INTELLIGENCE:
SHOE SIZE:
OBNOXIOUS RATING:
EVIL THOUGHTS:

Murder the Clown says that being a clown can be murder. "I'm a clown. I was *born* a clown," he says. "When my mother saw me, she burst out laughing. I don't understand why people say they like my funny makeup. I don't wear any makeup! Sometimes people are afraid of clowns. So I grab them by both ears, give them a fierce head-butt, and scream, 'DON'T BE AFRAID!' I guess I just like to help people."

Ready for more?

Why did Jonathan Chiller bring Andy back to HorrorLand? What *real* terrors does he have in store for him?

You'll have to wait for the answers. You won't know Chiller's secret plans until you read *all seven* of the new HorrorLand books.

More kids will soon "take a little Horror home with them." Sam Waters will be next. You'll meet Sam in Goosebumps HorrorLand #14: LITTLE SHOP OF HAMSTERS.

Then you'll be one step closer to the most terrifying HorrorLand adventure of them all!

Here's a chilling preview of

Let me start out by saying that I love animals. And I'm desperate to have a pet of my own.

I'm so desperate, I even enjoyed petting the werewolves in the Werewolf Petting Zoo at HorrorLand Theme Park.

Yes, there is a big pen outside Werewolf Village. You go inside, and you can pet the werewolves, rub their bellies, and scratch their furry backs.

A big sign says: JUST DON'T PUT YOUR HAND IN THEIR MOUTHS.

Pretty good advice.

Should I back up and tell you who I am and stuff like that? Sometimes, I get so *psyched* about animals I forget to do anything else.

My name is Sam Waters. I'm twelve, and so is my friend Lexi Blake. Lexi and I spent a week at HorrorLand, and we had some good, scary fun. Especially since our parents let us wander off on our own.

Lexi is tall and blond and kind of chirpy and giggly and *very* enthusiastic. I guess she comes on a little strong, but I'm used to her. We've been friends since we were three.

I'm not exactly the quiet type, either. My parents say that sometimes when Lexi and I get together, we're like chattering magpies. I've never seen a magpie, so I don't really know what they are talking about. I keep meaning to Google *magpies*. Maybe they make good pets.

I'm shorter than Lexi. Actually, I'm one of the shortest guys in the sixth grade. But I could still have a growth spurt, right?

I have short black hair and dark eyes, and my two front teeth poke out a little when I smile, just like my little brother, Noah.

Bunny teeth, Dad calls them. And then I always say, "Could I have a bunny for a pet?" He's so sick of me asking, he usually doesn't even answer. Just makes a groaning noise.

Anyway, it was a hot, sunny summer afternoon. Lexi and I walked out of the Werewolf Petting Zoo into the crowded park.

"Those werewolves were totally gross," Lexi said, wiping her hands on the sides of her dark green shorts. "Their fur was sticky, like they were sweating or something."

"I don't think wolves sweat," I said. "I think the bristles on their fur feel sticky because — HEY!"

Lexi pulled me out of the way of a rolling food cart. The side of the cart said: FAST FOOD. A green-and-purple Horror was chasing after it.

"They couldn't be real werewolves," Lexi said. "But they didn't look like regular wolves — did they?"

"They had human eyes," I said. "I mean . . . the way those werewolves looked at us. Like they were smarter than animals. And their fangs were longer than wolf fangs."

Lexi shivered. "You're creeping me out, Sam." She crinkled up her face. "They sure *smelled* like animals. Yuck. I can't get the smell out of my nose. They stank!"

I pinched my nose. "Are you sure it was the werewolves?"

She grabbed the park map from my hand and smacked me on the shoulder with it. We shoved each other back and forth playfully.

"Are you hungry?" she asked. "I'm hungry. Hungry enough to bite a werewolf!"

She snapped her teeth at me a few times. I had to push her away. "Down, girl! Down!"

I grabbed the map away from her. "Let's see where we are. There's probably a restaurant somewhere. . . ."

I unfolded the map and raised it to my face. The sun was so bright, I needed to squint to read it.

"Let me help," Lexi said. She tugged at the map — too hard — and ripped it in half. She burst out laughing. "Hey — I don't know my own strength!"

"Please don't help me," I groaned. "You're always trying to help me."

"What's the big deal, Sam?" she said. "You read your half and I'll read my half."

"We don't have to read the map," I told her. I pointed. "Look. That's a little restaurant right there."

We crossed the wide path and peeked into the open door. It was a lunch-counter place. Round red stools in front of a long yellow counter.

I read the sign beside the door. THE SPEAR-IT CAFÉ: IF YOU CAN SPEAR IT, YOU CAN EAT IT!

"Huh?" I read the sign again. "What does that mean? This doesn't sound too good."

"I don't care," Lexi said. She grabbed me around the waist and pushed me inside. "I'm starving. We're eating here."

I stumbled into the little restaurant. We took seats at the end of the counter.

And that's when all the trouble began.

About the Author

R.L. Stine's books are read all over the world. So far, his books have sold more than 300 million copies, making him one of the most popular children's authors in history. Besides Goosebumps, R.L. Stine has written the teen series Fear Street and the funny series Rotten School, as well as the Mostly Ghostly series, The Nightmare Room series, and the two-book thriller *Dangerous Girls*. R.L. Stine lives in New York with his wife, Jane, and Minnie, his King Charles spaniel. You can learn more about him at www.RLStine.com.

DOUBLE THE FRIGHT ALL AT ONE SITE

www.scholastic.com/goosebumps

FIENDS OF GOOSEBUMPS & GOOSEBUMPS HORRORLAND CAN:

- PLAY GHOULISH GAMES!
- CHAT WITH FELLOW FAN-ATICS!
- WATCH CLIPS FROM SPINE-TINGLING DVDs!
- EXPLORE CLASSIC BOOKS AND NEW TERROR-IFIC TITLES!
- CHECK OUT THE GOOSEBUMPS HORRORLAND VIDEO GAME!
- GET GOOSEBUMPS PHOTOSHOCK FOR THE IPHONE™ OR IPOD TOUCH®!

■ SCHOLASTIC

GBWEB

Goosebumps HorrorLand™

The Original Bone-Chilling

Series
—with Exclusive Author Interviews!